Praise for Emily Maguire's *An Isolated Incident*

**Shortlisted for the Miles Franklin Literary Award
and the Stella Prize**

'Superb writing and sense of place. Totally credible voices. Read her!'

Ann Cleeves, author of the Two Rivers series

'This hugely chilling and evocative story, mixing lyrical language and brutal events, is told with great psychological acuity'

Anita Sethi, author of *I Belong Here*

'A harrowing, fascinating, compelling work from an accomplished and thoughtful Australian writer who uses the vehicle of a young woman's death to question and explore society's treatment of women, the everyday violence it condones and its intrusive fascination with the murder of pretty young women'

Australian

'Utterly engrossing... Rather than creating a simple case of goodies and baddies, Maguire subtly examines the complexity of the human personality and what leads somebody to feel destructive. This hugely chilling and evocative story, mixing lyrical language and brutal events, is told with great psychological acuity'

Sydney Morning Herald

Emily Maguire is the author of seven novels, including *An Isolated Incident*, shortlisted for the Stella Prize and the Miles Franklin Literary Award in 2017, and *Love Objects*, shortlisted for the Australian Book Industry Awards Literary Fiction Book of the Year and the Margaret & Colin Roderick Literary Award in 2022, as well as three non-fiction books. Her articles and essays on sex, feminism and culture have been published widely including in the *Sydney Morning Herald*, the *Australian*, the *Observer* and the *Age*. Emily works as a teacher and as a mentor to young and emerging writers and was the 2023 H. C. Coombs Creative Arts Fellow at the Australian National University.

Also by Emily Maguire

FICTION

Taming the Beast

The Gospel According to Luke

Smoke in the Room

Fishing for Tigers

An Isolated Incident

Love Objects

NON-FICTION

Princesses and Pornstars

Your Skirt's Too Short

This is What a Feminist Looks Like

RAPTURE

EMILY MAGUIRE

Sceptre

First published in Great Britain in 2024 by Sceptre
An imprint of Hodder & Stoughton Limited
An Hachette UK company

1

Copyright © Emily Maguire 2024

The right of Emily Maguire to be identified as the Author of the Work has been asserted by her in accordance with the Copyright, Designs and Patents Act 1988.

All rights reserved. No part of this publication may be reproduced, stored in a retrieval system, or transmitted, in any form or by any means without the prior written permission of the publisher, nor be otherwise circulated in any form of binding or cover other than that in which it is published and without a similar condition being imposed on the subsequent purchaser.

All characters in this publication are fictitious and any resemblance to real persons, living or dead, is purely coincidental.

A CIP catalogue record for this title is available from the British Library

Hardback ISBN 9781399731065
Trade Paperback ISBN 9781399731089
ebook ISBN 9781399731072

Printed and bound in Great Britain by Clays Ltd, Elcograf S.p.A.

Hodder & Stoughton policy is to use papers that are natural, renewable and recyclable products and made from wood grown in sustainable forests. The logging and manufacturing processes are expected to conform to the environmental regulations of the country of origin.

Hodder & Stoughton Limited
Carmelite House
50 Victoria Embankment
London EC4Y 0DZ

www.sceptrebooks.co.uk

SOME SAY SHE WAS FROM MOGONTIACUM

(821-836)

THE ENGLISH PRIEST

HEAVEN IS NEVER-ENDING light. It is jasper and crystal, pearls and gold. It is lightning and rainbows and a great, rushing river. It is white horses and doves and angels singing holy holy holy and there is no sadness or pain, no hunger or thirst. Or there is hunger and thirst, but only to make the feasting tables, which are never bare, more pleasurable still. To get there you must be pious and humble and follow God's laws every day of your earthly life.

To the motherless five-year-old listening to such talk from beneath her father's table it does not seem worth the effort. Sweet as heaven might be, it cannot truly be better than life here and now in Mainz in the year 821. Could angel song truly be sweeter than the plainchant that floats down from the abbey on the hill and fills all the empty spaces in her chest? Are white doves truly more lovely than the woodland throstles with their pale, speckled bellies and gold-tinted wings? As for horses, they have those here, as well as lightning and rainbows and the mightiest of all rivers running through town. Pearls and jasper are unknowns, but she has seen crystal and gold and, though they are pretty, there is not much use to either.

And why would she wish for never-ending daylight when it is the coming of night that brings the greatest pleasure? As the day fades, the serving girls lay out platters of meat and bread and ale, and then men come through the door and take their place around the table, underneath which she is already settled. The packed-earth floor is worn smoother than marble here and heated so richly by the hearth fire that when she is finally dragged to bed she can serve as her own warming stone.

Truly, right here is all the heaven she needs, a girl-sized paradise ending where the rushes begin, their edges trampled flat by pairs of boots more often than not.

Sometimes the men sit long enough for the mud caked on their ankles to dry and she makes a game of guessing which clods will fall first. Sometimes a man jiggles his legs or stomps his feet and she must cover her nose and mouth to stop from breathing in his dirt. If the men are very drunk or very angry their legs might dance wildly about and she must stay alert or be kicked. If they are only a little drunk and feasting, then she may feast, too, on the scraps they drop unknowingly into her realm.

The men are merchants and traders, messengers and envoys, clerics and clergymen. They gossip and argue and bargain into the night at her father's table because he is a personal friend and confidant to the Archbishop, and—even a child knows this is not unrelated—a man of both influence and wealth. There are contracts and favours to be won, grudges to be supported, controversies to be quelled or fuelled. There is a long, solid table laid with good food and better ale.

Her father is known to all as the English Priest, although he speaks the common tongue as well as any Frank and hasn't performed the rites nor worn the stole since before her birth. But he hails from Wessex and came to the Continent in the missionary footsteps of his slain countryman St Boniface, so the English Priest he will always be.

On nights he forgets she is there, the daughter can hear tales of her father's early days in Francia. For almost three decades he travelled this land finding souls for God and King Charles, saving generations of Saxon babes from lives spent worshipping rocks and afterlives of eternal torment. He rode ahead of Charles's army, blessing whole towns that had warning from gore-splattered refugees of what was coming. On occasion he was barely in time, the soldiers' sweat already watering the ground on which the pagans fell to their knees and begged for baptism.

Not all accepted the proffered gift, preferring the sword to salvation. Even those, her godly father did his best for, praying for their eternal souls as their bodies bled out.

By Charles's death in 814, the work was all but finished. Most villages the English Priest passed through welcomed him and asked not only for a blessing but also for advice on raising a church of their own, on sacraments and saint days, on the rights and wrongs of proper Christian living. Though now and then he came upon people who held to the old ways, he found their reluctance easily shifted once he assured them they could still have their festivals and rituals so long as they used the rightful Christian names and replaced their idols with a simple cross.

In one of these still-pagan places, he saved the soul of the woman who would soon bear his child. Whether the saving happened before or after he lay on her was unclear. Given the exalted way in which the men at table talk about rutting, it may well have been during.

Her mother was an extraordinary beauty (a fact never mentioned around that table, only in the market and churchyard in order to lament that the child takes after her father, both of them pale and thin as discarded hay) and so nobody much blamed the English Priest for swiving her. There would be no retribution or bloodshed so long as he arranged a generous gift to the wounded family and went on his way. Perhaps even an annual stipend, given how valuable a marriage prospect he had ravaged. He refused, instead putting her in the back of his cart and driving to the nearest church to marry her himself.

Despite abandoning his calling, the English Priest was awarded a fine house in the centre of Mainz by the Archbishop in thanks for his service (and, it must be said, the thirty-seven *Karlspfund* of mysteriously acquired gold and silver he donated to the See). He had barely begun to enjoy his new wife and home before he received heavenly punishment in the form of an infant, tearing out with such haste and violence that the mother was dead before the priest had made it to the end of the street to call for some women to assist.

Once, when the English Priest was absent from the table, a man whispered that the cross around the dead wife's neck had a pagan symbol engraved on the side she wore against her skin. It were a hammer, someone said. No, said another, a likeness of the heathen tree that Blessed Boniface felled. In any case, it was known that the woman washing the body for burial turned the cross in her hands and was burnt. It was known, too, that the assisting girl replaced the polluted cross around the corpse's throat and, for allowing such a thing to enter consecrated ground, her own throat closed over and she never spoke again.

Later, the child asked her father if it were true her mother died unsaved. He clapped her head with both hands so her ears rang and rang and said it was a sin to listen to the gossip of fishwives. She did not tell him it was the gossip of the town's best and wisest men lest he rip her ears clean off her head.

WHAT SHE KNOWS

THE CHILD IS named Agnes after the saint who was once a girl who became a young woman who was burnt at the stake and stabbed in the throat for refusing the men who wished to lay on her. The child asked once if it might have been better for this woman to have lain under the men and then gotten up afterwards and still been alive. Her father did smile but said she mustn't say such things. The saints' lives were provided as holy instruction and so by definition there was no better way to live.

'And die,' Agnes said.

'Sometimes, yes.'

But Agnes knows they always die, the saints. And hardly ever without great pain.

She does not know it is odd for a girl to read until one of her father's guests, a Benedictine from Fulda Abbey, spots her bent over a book by the fire and roars as though he's spied a deer hunting a man.

No benefit and much harm derives from women reading, he tells her father, who responds that this man's own order is known to educate girls.

'Girls destined for the cloister, and even then I would have them learn their prayers and hymns by heart rather than risk corruption in this way.'

'The great Charles himself insisted on his daughters' educations.'

'Ah, yes,' the Benedictine says, 'those paragons of virtue.'

Her father purples and Agnes thinks he will wallop the monk. Instead he calls for more ale and turns the discussion to the successive bountiful harvests they've been blessed with up at the abbey.

She herself does not speak to the monk, does not look at him directly. She is eight years old and must not cry, but she was frightened of the man even before he seized her book and began to shout. Of all the men who pass through this house, only the Benedictines terrify her like this. Their hooded black robes are thicker and longer than any garment need be. They are designed to conceal, but what? Their voices, too, are low and secretive, except when they are—like this one—agitated, in which case they bellow as though expecting God Himself to heed them.

If she could bring herself to speak to the Benedictine, she would tell him that she has learnt more about sinners and their deeds and the evil that stalks the earth from staying silent beneath this table than could be contained in all the books of the great library of Fulda combined.

It is not from a book she has learnt, for example, that the fine and famous church in Frankfurt was built over the remains of a pagan child, daughter of a warrior lord. Alongside the tiny bones lay golden idols and burnt animal offerings to false gods. She knows, too, of the infant still marked by birth but already dead left outside the walls of Altmünster Abbey. Not in any book, that tale. The men at table agreed the babe could only have come from one of the nuns inside. It was well known they were a loose-living cohort there. One man proposed a delegation to examine every seal in the place to determine which had been broken. Another said that if reputation be a guide they would find most every door within had been opened—and well used at that. If reputation is a guide, a third man added, our delegation will be welcomed as a reward.

Her father silenced the ribaldry by telling of a case some years ago in which the abbess had her charges march around the convent walls singing Psalms, their arms outstretched in the shape of the cross. If one of them were guilty she would surely fall, but none did and the sight of the suffering and piety of these fine women of God inspired a local maid to at last confess to having borne and left the child.

'I would therefore advise,' her father finished, 'all those who seek to blame the holy sisters of the abbey to look first to their own cowardly and dishonest womenfolk.'

Something else Agnes learnt that night without reading a thing: men can beat half the life out of each other and then embrace as tender and loving brothers before the blood on the rushes has dried.

Only yesterday, and without touching a book, she learnt that at the northern edge of this very town, good people were having their rest disturbed by an invisible being hurling rocks at their walls. The men at table disagreed about whether the being were a revenant or demon, but most agreed a priest should be called to test it.

Her father, though, told of a village he visited where the local priest had tried to exorcise a spirit and had only made it bolder. Now it had voice and would drift about spreading rumours, creating discord and hatred among the villagers. Better that those affected here stay safely indoors at night and pray when they heard the rocks coming. Whatever the thing was, it would become bored at its lack of effect and soon head elsewhere for mischief.

The men yielded to his view as they most usually did, but Agnes saw the clenched fists on thighs, the agitated boots, that her father didn't. She knows from watching well (she wishes she could tell the Benedictine) that men might say one thing with their mouths while their bodies said another thing altogether.

While the Benedictine and her father continue to talk of harvests, Agnes flees through the back door, past the cook and serving girl sweating over their pots, and secretes herself in the furthest corner of the kitchen garden. It will soon be dark; the monk will go to his prayers and other men will come, and there will be ale and stew and scraps of secrets.

A fennel shoot between her teeth and freshly turned soil between her toes, she pokes at the cabbage patch looking for worms and beetles. But all the crawling, flying things have gathered by the hole in the fence to the yard next door. Agnes picks her way across, careful not to noticeably tread on the leeks or chard lest she get noticeably smacked by the cook.

A kitten, stretched as though seeking the sun on its soft pale belly. A perfect darling thing except for the gash in its side, about which the insects are making such a fuss. Agnes shoos away the flying things, though they hover just beyond her hand, ready to rejoin the crawlers the moment she lets down her guard.

She knows kittens die. Most of them drowned before their eyes are fully opened to a world with no use for them. The odd one kept to replace an old mouser that has lost its hunger. She has always known this fact.

To know is not to understand. She strokes the pale belly and it is not soft as it should be, nor warm. It is as cold and hard as the fence. As dead as. Not a kitten at all.

Dead means you are not what you were. It means you are not.

Does her father know this? He must, yet how does he go on?

Each day she returns to the thing that was a kitten and sees it become less itself. Become more a smell. More a feast for other creatures. More a borderless patch of fur and guts sinking into the yard. The very ground on which she sleeps, walks, eats is filled with messes like that. They used to do the same as her, every one of them, and now they rot piece by piece, their flesh sliding into soil.

Among them is her nimbed mother, who she never met but whose name is sacred. How—she asks the Lord as she lies awake in something worse than terror—how will my mother know me in heaven with her eyes turned to water in her skull? Her skull perhaps, by that time, water too. My mother, soon my father. I! All of us turned to muck and then nothing at all.

The meat on the table is no different to that decaying underfoot, no different to the substance of her. She cannot touch it, repulsed by the thought of making more of her flesh by ingesting that of others. Her father orders her to eat what is served. She refuses. He rages. It has no effect. The imaginings of the darkest hours are far worse than anything his soft human hands can do.

Her father forbids her from reading, banishes her to bed before the guests arrive.

After a week of this, she eats a tranche of mutton. 'The child is a born monk,' the English Priest crows. 'Deprives herself of every comfort so long as she can still study her tracts.'

Soon after, flooding rain rips trees and crops from the earth and joins half the houses and all inside them with the rushing Rhine. For days the drowned, human and animal both, bob on rivers newly made of the streets. When at last the rains slow enough for the living to venture out and collect the dead, they find coffins wrenched from the churchyard, split open on tree roots and stones and roofs, and so, among the recent dead sodden with water and filth, are corpses in every state of decomposition.

Death, so recently revealed as the most unfathomable horror, has become an ordinary foulness.

THE HEART OF CHRISTENDOM

THE CITY THEY called Mainz had once been the Roman military stronghold of Mogontiacum and the capital of Germania Superior. Her father has shown her where the Roman wall once ran parallel to the Rhine. Walking past the warehouses that line the road, waiting to be filled with wares coming up and down the river, and the workshops making goods to be loaded onto those same boats, Agnes flutters her eyes open and closed and sees the hulking stone wall and the soldiers in their burnished breastplates. She has never seen a Roman wall or a soldier or a breastplate, yet when she flutters her eyes there they are.

Her father does not like her to dwell on the Roman times. She should turn her thoughts to what followed: the coming of

Clovis, the pagan king who converted to the true faith and, with God on his side, united the Frankish tribes. Agnes cannot conjure up images of Clovis and his soldiers the way she can the Romans. She doesn't know if the men wore armour at all, let alone burnished plates on their chests. She would like to see an illustration of Clovis on the day he became Christian. She would like to see him kneeling beside his wife, Clothilde, who was Christian first and the one who brought him to God.

It would not be wrong, Agnes thinks, to say that Clothilde is responsible for the millions of saved souls for which her husband is praised. It would not be wrong, but it would be unwise, as men prefer their female saints sacrificial rather than heroic. She learnt this beside, rather than beneath, her father's table when she failed to stop herself interjecting that it was Brunhilda of Austrasia who rebuilt and strengthened the western empire of the Franks while Clovis's male progeny bickered and warred.

'As you know so much, I suppose you know how that vengeful old cow was ended?' her father said, and the gathered men became the cheering crowd and Agnes that great queen, tied across wild horses and torn apart when those creatures did as they must and ran free.

Whoever is to thank for it all, the fact is that by the time Agnes was born, Mainz was the heart of the Christian peoples throughout the blessed and glorious Frankish kingdom. At her father's table it is said that the Archbishop, one of the seven men in the entire empire responsible for selecting the emperor (and, never forget, her father's very close personal friend), is second only to the Bishop of Rome when it comes to holiness and power. Indeed, as most Franks will never in their lifetimes travel south of the Alps, let alone all the way to Rome, the Archbishop of Mainz *is* Holiness and Power. Most would not know the difference, her father says, between our cathedral church and St Peter's in Rome, and so one may as well be the other.

Mainz, then, is the most important place in the world for many of the ten million or so inhabitants of the empire. In daylight, while her father visits other men of influence, this place—the most important in the world—is Agnes's playground. The riverfront road with its imagined wall and soldiers, yes, but also the alleys and lanes between and behind the warehouses, the maze of the town proper with its wooden churches scattered everywhere, like toy versions of the Archbishop's stone church. The endless clutter of stalls, some trading in a speciality like incense or candles, others selling whatever has come to them via the river traders, so that you may buy from the one stall, on any given day, a cake of Spanish soap, a coil of rope and the desiccated toe of a desert saint. And behind the stalls, the shophouses where the wealthier merchants live and trade, most of them having at least a few chickens or geese, if not a clutch of pigs or sheep, cluttering up the yards and air. The clucking and bleating, snorting and scratching drowned out most of the day by the chatter and calling, singing and ranting of their owners, buyers, caretakers, eaters.

Her father is not the only man known by his place of birth in this city of immigrants and wayfarers. Indeed, in the thickest tangle of town you would be hard pressed to find a person born within a week's hard ride. Anyone travelling between Albion or Hibernia and Rome will pass through Mainz, as will those coming from the north and east. Many stay only long enough to empty or fill their wagons or boats, but others find it suits them to remain in a place where most every language is spoken, every type of stew or bread made. And although the Roman churches and abbeys outnumber the Irish, the latter are still found here, and both kinds are home to clergy and monks from all over Christendom.

The girls who serve at her father's table are sometimes from one of the nearby villages and sometimes from further north or east. Always they are young and pretty, and rarely does one stay long enough for Agnes to learn her ways or even her name.

Sometimes there are other children to play with, though their liberty comes and goes with the demands of trade and harvest. The only child as free from obligation as Agnes is Frix, whose mother also died in birthing and whose father, the night-watchman, sleeps all day. Frix is the same age and height as her, and when they play Beasts they are too evenly matched. It is supposed to be a fight to the death, but they both choose lion and their clawing and rolling goes on and on without either giving in. Often she comes home scratched and bruised, her clothing caked in mud, her hair thickened by dust and grass. Her father does not mind, though sometimes a serving girl or the cook will notice and shout at her to wash.

In her tenth year her father gives her a copy of the most spectacular Bestiary and, as Frix cannot read, it is up to Agnes to explain to him the varied strengths and weaknesses of the animals. Lions, for example, are killed instantly by brambles! It is madness for them to continue to choose such an easily killed beast.

The peacock, on the other hand, is immortal, which should make it fun to play, but it is also very weak and without battle skills. A contest with anything other than a worm or rat would go forever and without the satisfaction of lion to lion brawling.

The elephant need only place her foot on any part of her enemy and say stomp and he has to fall to the ground as though crushed. Her weakness is not having knees; if she falls she cannot rise again.

The panther looks fierce, but is truly the sweetest of all beasts, with fragrant breath that attracts other animals to him irresistibly. When Frix takes this form Agnes cannot help running to him and begging to smell his breath, and he obliges, puffing all over her face until the two of them are one hot bundle of laughter.

They are blissful panther and peacock one warm, sweet-smelling afternoon in late September and all at once Frix's father, out on midday business instead of asleep as he should be, is hauling them up by their shifts, smacking their legs until they're red as mouths. He drags them each by one ear through town, and though Agnes is sent outside she hears the nightwatchman tell the English Priest that he should not allow his daughter to roll around in the woods like a little heathen. Some stains cannot be removed by even the most powerful of friends, he says.

Her tapping at Frix's window goes unanswered. She finds him playing with the other children near her own favourite bramble patch and all of them shun her.

She runs past them to the edge of the forest proper, pauses. All her life she has been told to be afraid of what lurks beyond: madmen and bandits and murderous Northmen, says her father. Fauns and snatchers and headless riders, say the market wives.

Agnes will take snatchers and fauns over the blank stares of Frix. She'll happily risk the bandits and Northmen—perhaps she will even join them!—rather than dirty her knees crawling back to those infants.

She breathes deep and straightens her spine and treads deliberately past the tree line. Like in the *vitas* when a saint ascends to heaven, the crude and loud human world is gone, immediately forgotten. She is done with all that, has found the place she belongs. She lies on the soft, thick mat of gold and red, sees that the beech trees above have somehow held on to more than they have given to the ground, each pale trunk surrounded by a cloud of leaves in colours any king would envy for his throne. Her eyes flutter open and closed and she can believe that wood sprites are making the light dance through the branches just for her.

Soon the cold begins to seep from the ground into her bones; she runs further into her realm, begins to climb. Here the trees are older even than the Roman ruins, their trunks like the legs of giants cast in stone. When Boniface came upon the Hessians worshipping an oak he swung his axe into the trunk and God showed whose side He was on by bringing the whole mighty tree down at once. It is a puzzle to her that God would destroy an oak to show His power when already He had shown much greater power by making the tree and all around it. To destroy is so easy in comparison.

RAPTURE

—

In the holy month she falls ill and her father hires a woman to keep her inside through the winter. She would not mind so much but his guests are fewer in these months and no new books arrive. Her mind is like a cave; her own thoughts echo endlessly, become strange and terrible in their loneliness.

She returns to her forest and is greeted by a litter of four striped and impish piglets. She feeds them bread from her pockets and, soon, whether she is swinging from a branch or lain flat by the stream, they find her and nestle their oddly soft noses into whatever part of her they can reach, nudge her into stroking them. They run ahead and dart back to make sure she follows, care nothing for the paths forged by traders or grazing sheep, tramping as easily through dense shrubs as slippery sedge. The trees marked by honey hunters are the same to them as those that have never been lopped and boarded. Agnes imitates them, moves low to the ground, nuzzles and sniffs and rolls. She becomes accustomed to the smell of decomposing leaves, is comforted to catch it clinging to her hair in bed at night.

For hours at a time she lies still enough that the forest forgets to be wary and she is allowed to see the gold-splotched lizards the size of her thumb that crawl out from beneath fallen bark.

She comes to know the precise sound of missile thrush tapping their beaks, the air rippled by a wagtail bobbing, the scent of earth freshly turned by worms on the move.

She lies still and she talks with God. It is not prayer. That is a ritual performed at home on her knees or in a church, its object distant and disinterested. In the forest God is as close and real as the bark and the leaves. He moves through her with every breath of loamy air.

April and the forest is as busy and bright as the town on market day. Purple and pink and white blossoms feasted on by fattening bees and butterflies wearing the costumes of new apples and bluebells. A grasshopper alights on a fresh green branch, all transparent wings and delicate, pretty hands that appear to close in prayer before it too flies away. Ah! God is a merry prankster indeed, to allow a creature out of the pagan fairy stories to thrive right here in His Christian forest.

Sweet snuffling at her feet and Agnes bends to scoop up her piglets, sees they have lost their stripes, outgrown her hands. She cries out like her father has clapped her ears. Her sweet friends will soon be murderous beasts. Already their bodies hard-muscled enough to bring down a dog. Or a child. She scuffs at the ground, shouts *shoo shoo shoo* but they think it all a game, gambol behind, in front, around her legs. Furious, she kicks at the largest, sends it skidding through the brittling leaves. All four scamper, squealing at her betrayal.

This is no merry prank but a cruel trick. Disguising killers as sweet babies. Dear God, my friend, your mischief will get me killed.

EXCEPTIONAL

TOMORROW THE ENGLISH Priest leaves for Fulda Abbey. Agnes approaches him at the table where he is bent over a ledger, asks if she may accompany him. She will be no trouble; quite the contrary. She can prepare his food along the way, take her turn driving the cart so he may rest.

Her father does not appear to have heard, continues striking his pen through this then that line of text. She goes on regardless. Surely, surely, he must know she has read every one of the books in this house a dozen times, can recite every page from memory. If only she can have a day—a morning, even—in the great library of Fulda, she will be more grateful than any child, more humble and obedient than any servant. She will—

'Stop, child. The road is no place for a girl. Nor is a monastery.'

'Father, please. I will go mad if I have nothing to do save mending and helping Cook. You must know—'

'Indeed, it is time we considered your future. I have held off on contracting your marriage, though the offers have been many. It is time.' He looks up from his ledger long enough to meet her eyes, nod with the weight of his decision. 'When I return from this visit, it will be time.'

She is not worried. The saints all have in common an exceptional childhood, and at twelve she is old enough to understand that this is what hers has been. Born to a great warrior of the faith, a man who ventured alone through barbarian territory, saving souls for God and winning hearts for Charles the Great. Her father, a young foreign priest carrying no weapon yet emerging unscathed and triumphant from the Saxon wars. This righteous and holy man who did not hand her to the nuns at birth as all around him urged. A motherless child—and a daughter at that! Madness to keep her, and then he went ahead and raised her to read and think better than most men. He has boasted himself of this daughter who knows more of the faith and the church than many bishops. He has not taken all this trouble only to let her go to some witless young cleric or newly moneyed town dullard.

—

He returns from Fulda with not a single new book for her to read, only a swathe of pale-green northern linen she is to sew into a long tunic, and a ribbon of russet silk to gild it. He presents these to her as though they are gifts, and she is obliged to tell him that dressing like a maiden will not make her one.

'You must know, Father, I do not intend to be married.'

'Do you not indeed? The convent for you, is it?'

It is a joke he enjoys casting. Convents are for the excess daughters of the nobility, high-born ladies too ugly, old or far down the line to make useful marriages. Those rare women called to service and allowed to enter without wealth are costumed housemaids. Lower than housemaids, given that those they serve are so often other nuns.

'I think that I might, in fact. I think I should make a fine abbess. I would—'

'There is no such creature as a fine abbess.' His voice tells her he still thinks it all a joke.

She prays that God will send a clear sign of her destiny. Like the veil He placed over Austrebertha's reflection in the river. Better still if He puts the vision in front of her father's eyes, that *he* be made to see her proper path.

Months pass with no prophetic vision, no sign from God. Only increasing demands from her father that she eat more, fill herself out. She is ordered to stand with the women at church and to mark how they dress and speak and generally comport themselves. At home, she is forbidden from sitting under the table and nor may she sit at it with the men. She is to help the serving girl with her tasks and then retire to her bed, where she may read as long as a single candle stub allows.

One such night, as her light trembles to its end, there is a battering on the door, a shout for women to help with a birth gone too long. Cook says she will bring both girls and it takes a moment for Agnes to understand she is included in this. She waits for her father to protest, but he nods and returns to his conversation.

Wind and rain lash them as they run—sliding here, slipping there—to a house in an alley off the riverfront. House is not the right word. In her own bed, Agnes had barely known the storm was about; a pleasant drumming on the roof, a vague awareness that in-here had been made sweeter by contrast with out-there. In this not-house, this single room with loose dirt floors, a hearthless fire and a thin pallet of straw on which a woman in a bloodied shift screams and screams—here, the storm is all but inside with them. The wind barely gentled by the walls; the roof creaking its own terror.

There are too many people in this loud and wavering room. The call for women went out and, despite the late hour and the storm, here they are. Agnes recognises none. They are wives of fishermen and merchants, she supposes. Laundresses and mat weavers and pot scrubbers. Cook and the serving girl dissolve into the mass, become part of this one body with many hands and voices, all working together to soothe, to wipe, to command. In the centre of it all, the mother thrashes as though the devil himself is tossing her about for fun.

Agnes presses her back against the shuddering wall, slides to the ground. She wishes for the house to collapse, for the wind to be louder than the screams, for the rain to drown the smell of blood and shit that fills her nostrils. She scrapes her palms against the floor, presses them to her face, but the dirt is no match for this stench.

The wailing stops suddenly as though the throat it came from has been cut.

The woman on the pallet will not be heard again. Her body is nothing but a torn relic, her soul already in flight.

Agnes watches the women do their grim work. It is a few moments before she understands that there have been two lives lost and only one soul lifted high. The tiny, blue babe the woman fought to bring forth all these long, terrible hours cannot follow her to the final and glorious rest in heaven. Yet how could that mother be at peace herself, knowing her child is gone to nothingness?

She doesn't notice when the storm ends, but as she walks home through the dawn-brushed town she thinks the air has never smelt cleaner, the light never been so lovely. The feeling in her is, perhaps, more than she can bear.

At home her father scolds her for wetting the floor, dragging in mud and the Lord only knows what else.

Mats laid barely a week and already filthy. He is chewing yesterday's bread, and if he says a word about the absence of Cook and the serving girl, Agnes will set the table alight and him with it.

She walks past him and out the back door, where she scrubs her hands and the hem of her dress. The other women will need to soak their garments for a week to remove the gore. She is a soldier returning from battle with tunic as clean as it started.

When she re-enters the house her father does not glance in her direction, only tells her she must collect fresh rushes to lay over the mats until they can be beaten clean. There are important guests this evening and slovenliness will not do.

She drinks from the jug on the table. The small ale is past its best but as good as fresh picked mint in her sour mouth.

'Did you not hear me, child? Go!'

'Forgive me, Father. I am very tired. The birthing was—'

'Stop your mouth, girl. There will be no talk of such things in my house.'

Tell the women their washcloths and oils will be needed again, Agnes thinks. Tell the hangman he'll soon have a murderer to hoist. Whether it's Agnes today and her father tomorrow or the other way, she does not care. Her hatred for him and the world both is entire.

'How fortunate you are, Father, to command silence when you wish it. If only I had such power last night. I may have been spared the sound of a woman being torn apart from the inside as—'

'Enough!' His eyes are closed, his hands press the open book into the table. 'I am spared nothing, have lived with that sound in my head every day of your life.'

The hatred drains. He is only a man and has borne more than most in her birth and keeping.

She puts on her cloak, collects her basket from the back door. 'Forgive me, Father,' she says. 'I will go now for the rushes. I will get for you some honey cake as well, I think.'

Still he doesn't look up. Says, 'Take some yourself, while you're about it. You'll be half starved by now, I expect.'

The day has turned hot and still, as though God, too, is worn out by the wet and wind of last night. The usual morning stench of emptied piss pots, fish guts and slaughtered fowl have no breeze to disperse them. She cannot bring herself to enter the market, strides clean past it, on to the edge of town and into her forest.

RAPTURE

The air here is cool and scented with pine needles scattered by the tempest. She is grateful for it but her mind will not be so easily cleansed. She does not know the name of the woman she saw die last night, does not know what she looked like when not dying. She thinks of Sophy, the butcher's daughter, who died birthing last spring. Sophy, who was barely older than Agnes and unmarried, and whose dying bellows were said to have reached all the way to the Archbishop's chambers, though Agnes lives much closer and heard nothing. The market wives said that the thing slid from Sophy had hooves and long teeth. It was known the girl bent over for her father's carthorse, so there was no fear of devilry in this case. Besides, the poor beast was born dead and the devil's children are always born hearty, though they sicken and die within weeks.

Agnes didn't need to be there to know it wasn't the devil nor laying with a carthorse that killed Sophy. It was the same thing that killed the woman last night, killed Agnes's own mother and many others besides. And what of those it didn't kill? Near every woman between fourteen and thirty treated worse than a milking cow, heaving through endless chores only to disappear for a month to recover from the shit-smeared body-tearing act of birth. And then, if she was lucky, she would return to the world for a brief bout of work before her breeding time began again. Or was returning the fate of the unlucky? She is not sure at all.

It is said a boy can avoid war by lopping off a finger or toe. What part of me, Agnes wonders, might I sever to be freed from the bloody service required of girls?

A rich, musky scent accompanies her for some minutes before its meaning arrives and the hair on her limbs bristles as though she, too, is a boar preparing to charge. Before she fully understands that the dark cluster of shrubs in front of her has transformed into muscle, bone and tusks, her body reacts, turns and runs along the just-trodden path.

Poor frightened animal body that does what it can while the knowing mind takes its time. *Stand your ground and shout with authority*, her mind says as the back of her thigh bursts open and the rest of her flips in the air and comes down hard. *Play dead*, her clever, too-slow mind instructs as her body scrambles for the nearest tree. The boar backs up, lowers its monstrous head. Her hands cling heroically to the branch as a tusk slides through her guts, then out again. The boar moves away, hooves the dirt. Its next charge will gore her all the way to heaven.

At last God takes her side, allays the pain for as long as it takes to hoist herself fully onto the branch. She lies like a hunting cat as the boar grunts its frustration at having lost its prey. Soon it lumbers away through the bushes and Agnes breathes deeply of air that no longer carries its musk.

Was her impaler one of the darlings who snuffled her belly as she lay in the leaf litter beneath this very tree? Was this punishment for abandoning them once they were no longer babes? If not that, what? Something must have caused this astonishing violence.

Her mind stops searching as her body stops trying to be anything other than still. Her blood keeps moving, though, painting the bough and feeding the soil well into the night, when the search party her father raises finds what they think is a murdered child hidden in the thick middle branches of the forest's oldest oak.

Awake but somehow not. Pain that cannot be real. Days and nights like this, knowing and unknowing. Father murmuring and ladies praying, hot stones pressing her down and the overwhelming smell of salt brine as though she is being preserved for the season along with the excess radish crop.

Clarity returns little by little over the coldest months. Each time her father leaves her side he presses her hand to his lips and promises he will return at speed. Women come and go. Strangers treat her body as if it were their most precious possession. She does not like being lifted, turned, handled. Does not like being bathed like a babe or having potions painted over her middle and held in place with stones for hours.

When her wounds are at last dry and hard, and she can sit by herself and spoon pottage into her own mouth, she hears her father in furious discussion with some visiting men and she understands that a marriage contracted mere weeks before her injury has been cancelled.

She pretends to sleep and learns from the women attending her that people think the English Priest quite mad. The lengths the man has gone to in order to save his daughter and for what? All knew she was a wild and undisciplined child, leaf- and twig-littered, solitary and often heard speaking to herself. All knew her mother was a pagan until death. Now the child's flesh matches her blood. What parents would knowingly invite such a cursed creature into their family? What future could a motherless, maimed and unmarriageable girl have? What use could she be to anyone, even a mad old Englishman?

With full heart and lifted spirit Agnes thanks God, who had, of course, been with her all along in the forest. He knew the depth of her suffering and fear and sent a beast to do the only thing that could save her. She will live and die unwanted by men; that is, free. And one day people will kneel at the tree that held her, will press their foreheads to the bloodstained trunk and give thanks for the day their beloved saint was spared.

NO ORDINARY BENEDICTINE

HER SCARS GROW with her; her stomach at thirteen, fourteen, fifteen, sixteen remains more purple than not, the skin there more gnarled than smooth. She cannot properly see the wound on the back of her thigh, but she can feel it: a jagged circle of gristle. It, too, refuses to give ground as her limbs lengthen.

Thirteen, fourteen, fifteen, sixteen. She must take down her hem every few months, gather up ever more parchment-coloured hair. Her father says she must stop growing soon or he will need to go begging in order to keep her shod.

It is a joke she does not recognise at thirteen. At fourteen she learns the household accounts and at fifteen takes sole responsibility for the outgoings. By sixteen she still doesn't understand what her father does to earn coin, but she knows the oak box he has kept in the bed chamber for as long as she can remember can barely hold it all. When he comments on the expense of the wool-lined boots she had made for them both she responds by offering to buy instead a larger coffer for all his silver.

At sixteen she no longer fears the Benedictines with their great black dresses and tonsured hair. When one or more come to the house she is bored. She pities them. Men with access to the best library on the Continent, men led by the celebrated Hrabanus Maurus, yet their minds are tiny water wheels marking off each cog in turn: no meat, twice-watered wine, here is the business I am to conduct on behalf of the abbot, truly I must go as it is time for prayer. It seems they must pray a dozen times a day and all at once, kneeling shoulder to shoulder in their cold stone church.

There is another of these bores coming for dinner this night, and her father is unusually excited. They have met before, the English Priest and this Brother Randulf, though Agnes does not know where or why. She only knows that her father, a man who dines regularly in the Archbishop's chambers and needs a dedicated ledger to keep track of his own schedule of dinner guests, has reserved this night for a single monk. Too, he has hired an extra serving girl, had the cook prepare a month's worth of stores in a day. Agnes imagines the old table creaking and cracking under the weight, the pork and barley, cheese and nuts and fruit and bread tipped onto the floor, which has been painstakingly refreshed that morning and so is quite clean enough to eat from in any case.

'All this for a Benedictine,' she says.

'No ordinary Benedictine,' her father replies, hovering near the door. 'Barely of age and for close to a decade reputed as Fulda's most skilled and prolific scribe. He's lately shown remarkable acumen for business and been given the rare privilege of travel to acquire new works for the abbey.'

Agnes smiles mildly, continues poking the fire. It is the first day of spring and already warm as high summer, but her father feels the cold more acutely of late. His bones, she fears, are ever closer to the air. He eats and eats but still his flesh recedes.

The door opens at last and the expected figure enters and embraces her father like a brother. They hold each other, exclaiming with pleasure at being reunited. Finally the Benedictine straightens, throws off his hood and turns to her.

'Agnes. It is a joy to finally meet you, dear sister.' He smiles like a hundred-year-old good Christian on his deep, soft death bed.

She is unable to speak—not that she should, being that this monk is her father's guest and she only here to help serve. Still, she feels the monk's eyes ask her to speak. Ask something of her, anyway. She does the only thing she knows to do: takes his cloak and lays it on a chair beside the fire so it will be warm for him on leaving.

Three years her senior, Brother Randulf has the bearing of a man, which Agnes sees now is different from that of both boy and monk. On him the voluminous costume might as well be a cavalryman's cloak. Without the tonsure you might not know he was a monk at all, and even that is less severe, less obvious than on others. His russet curls, longer than any she's seen on a man of cloth and perhaps tousled by the walk, fall softly over his forehead and cheeks.

When they sit to eat, Brother Randulf asks that Agnes join them and her father does not hesitate to nod his assent. Brother Randulf smiles at her and continues to smile as he helps himself to the thickest tranche of pork on the pile.

Agnes and her father eat little and say almost nothing as Brother Randulf gorges on plate after plate of fatty meat in between speaking of palaces and kings, pilgrims and saints, libraries hidden beneath crypts and books held in the arms of the incorruptible dead. When he speaks of the Holy Father in Rome it is as though he's just now broken bread with him at the wayside inn. When he speaks it is in a voice that belongs in a cathedral church. At the front, on high, leading them all.

'Forgive me,' he says, when all the ale and most of the food is gone. 'I fear I have worn your ears thin with all my talk.'

'There is nothing to forgive, brother. Few men have travelled so far and even fewer men of God. It is a privilege to hear from one who has seen the world without being tempted to join it.'

Brother Randulf looks at Agnes then, fast as a sparrowhawk strike. It is a look that says, *What a sweet fool is this English priest.* It says, *As though the world could tempt me when I am the thing that tempts the world.*

'Nevertheless,' he says to her father, who is fussing with the ale jug and has seen nothing, 'it is good of you to listen so. I do believe the only reason Abbot Hrabanus chose me for these missions is that he was tired of ordering penances for my inability to keep the silence.'

Her father laughs, upsets the jug, which is anyway empty. 'More ale, child,' he says. 'And then to bed with you.'

She stands to fetch the ale but Brother Randulf raises a hand. 'I must decline, good as it is. The porter on the hill thinks himself St Peter at the gates of heaven. He will cast me to the purgatory of ditch sleeping if he detects an ale-ward wobble.'

Agnes turns to leave as her father has ordered.

'Ah, but wait, sister. Sit with us a while longer,' the monk says. 'With your consent, of course, Brother English?'

Her father nods and so she sits, heart pulsing in her throat.

'The worst consequence of my gabbling is that I so often leave a room without hearing from the most interesting person within and then must spend the rest of my night in regret. Allow me, sister, to avoid this misery tonight at least.'

She looks to her father who regards the monk as though, like the disciples of Ephesus, he speaks a jumble of foreign tongues.

'Your father has told me,' Brother Randulf continues, as though it as an ordinary thing to speak directly to the daughter of a priest like she is your fellow, 'that you read as well as any man schooled by the monastics.'

Her father is pink-faced and so, she fears, is she.

'I do not wish to embarrass you, sister. Be calm. I only wish to know your thoughts on a matter discussed at every table throughout the empire: the edicts of Theophilus.'

'My daughter does not concern herself with politics, brother.'

'Forgive me, Brother English. I would not wish to suggest she might or should. But our Byzantine friend claims his edict banning images of our saints is biblical, while all I speak to in Italy and Francia claim the reverse. As someone who knows her Bible better than most, I believe Sister Agnes could steer us well.'

Her heart has set her throat on fire. In a breath or two she will be ash. Yet she inhales and exhales and remains a girl, whole and uncharred. Icons, is it? Well.

'Did God not instruct Moses,' she begins, and no flames flick from her tongue, 'to carve cherubim on the sacred ark, to weave their images on the curtains of the tabernacle?'

The monk and the priest lean forward on their elbows. The child beneath the table takes her place as a man above, and by the end of the night feels she has never been anything else.

Brother Randulf passes through Mainz once, twice, three times per month. Always he dines with the English Priest. Always he is the only guest and always he asks that Agnes join them. By the end of her seventeenth year she no longer waits for the invitation. It is the new order of things that on the nights Brother Randulf visits she sets herself a place at the table along with those of the men.

Sometimes Brother Randulf comes during the day and suggests Agnes join him for a walk. Sometimes there are errands to complete, his or hers or both. Often they merely wander through the market, down to the river, up the hill to the abbey where he sleeps while he is in Mainz.

As they walk, he tells her of handling thousand-year-old scrolls in the libraries of St Gall and Reichenau Abbey, of praying on the ground where St Benedict knelt at Monte Cassino, breaking bread with the ancient abbot who rebuilt the monastery centuries after the Lombards burnt it to the ground, a summer spent in the vivarium copying texts known to have been studied by Cassiodorus himself.

Agnes understands she rests upon a mountain top and all below is shrouded by cloud. When Randulf speaks the clouds clear, patch by patch. Look! There is Italy, a real place with churches in which to worship, gardens in which to plant seeds, roads on which to walk. And there! A shimmering lake where you might hear plainchant and holy bells as you row across to an abbey with a guesthouse, a vineyard, a scriptorium, a tower to climb up and view it all. Oh, there! A mountain pass over which pilgrims and traders traipse like ants on dropped bread, stopping to drink from streams as clear as the air, to pray in grottos bearing the knee prints of the blessed saints who sheltered there between revelation and martyrdom.

He talks and the clouds part. She sees paths the precise width of her tread winding soft and easy through the world entire.

On a cold, grey afternoon they reach the edge of the forest and she tells Brother Randulf of her months spent wild as a deer, how easy it seemed to be close to God. That the forest feels like it *is* God.

'You have read Tacitus?' Randulf asks.

'I have not.'

'He writes of the old people of this place, that *they consecrate woods and groves, and apply the names of deities to that hidden presence which is seen only by the eye of reverence.*'

'Oh.' The old people. Pagans. Her mother, perhaps. 'It is wrong, I know, Brother Randulf. I will try to correct it in myself. Only . . .' She looks to the top of the pines marking the town boundary. 'When I am in there, among them, it is hard not to think the birds and animals are as important to God and His plans as we ensouled humans. It seems—and I know the arrogance of this, brother—it seems as though God Himself is showing me my place as . . . as an equal piece, no more or less, in His creation.'

'I will bring you Tacitus to read,' Brother Randulf says, not angered by her blasphemy. Not even concerned, it seems. 'And Lucretius. Ah, yes, *De rerum natura*. You will enjoy it greatly, I believe.'

'My father only allows me to read Christian books.'

Brother Randulf turns to her, smiles in that way of his, like nothing in the world is or ever has been wrong. Never could be. 'A book kept in the greatest library in Christendom, under stewardship of the holy and venerated Hrabanus and lent to you by a Benedictine brother of Christ? It could not be more Christian if Jesus himself was the scribe.'

She laughs, shocked. Covers her mouth. He laughs then, too,

and it is a better sound than all the bells of all the churches in Francia.

He brings her the book by Tacitus. When it is time to return it to Fulda he leaves one by Lucretius in its place. Replaces Lucretius with Virgil and Virgil with Cicero.

Thus she learns that great and wise men felt as she had as a child on the forest floor. She learns there are systems of morality based on reason rather than God's will. She learns that women are useless and feeble but also, sometimes, worth fighting generationally long wars over. She learns that the northern Germanic people (her mother's people, perhaps, perhaps) were once ruled by women and ruled well. She learns that the monks of Fulda can read most anything they like and call it Christian work. She learns that Brother Randulf believes that she can too.

She is captivated by the ancient stories in the books Brother Randulf brings, but even more so by the recent history he narrates as they walk through Mainz. When he speaks of the Christianisation of Francia it is different from when her father and his friends tell it. With them, the old men, the stories are likewise old. The living flesh long fallen from the dry and yellow bones. Brother Randulf's stories are as fresh as his pink cheeks, his unlined hands. When he explains how the Saxons and Frisians were brought to God, she feels them around her on this very land. She feels them *inside her.*

'My mother was a Saxon,' she dares. 'A pagan.'

He nods. He knows more than Agnes does about everything. Even this. 'Your mother died a Christian,' he says, and it is honey drizzled over a decade-long itch.

'Still, it's strange to think how easily I might have been born a pagan.'

'It is not hard to imagine,' he says. 'You are the least civilised Christian I know.'

Heat rushes through her. She stops there in the middle of the road, sees he is looking at her with great affection, that he is teasing in the way men do with each other. The rush of heat becomes a warm bath.

'I suppose it is why we speak to each other so easily,' she says, and he claps his hand on her back, laughing. They are brothers in merry congress and it is the fulfilment of something she didn't know to wish for.

The week of her eighteenth birthday they walk by the river. He regrets he has no gift for her. The Rule of St Benedict does not allow brothers to own even the clothes on their backs.

She does not need anything from him save these conversations, she tells him.

'As a child, I dreamt of a life spent reading and thinking and talking about the things I read and thought. I prayed for God to mark me in a way my father could not deny. I prayed to be exceptional, like Austrebertha or Scholastica.'

Brother Randulf gestures to a patch of grass caught in the full beam of the morning sun. They sit, and he tells her that as a child he thought the kind of life she was describing a terrible misfortune. He had entered the monastery *pueri oblati*, the tenth child of a landholding family who might be rich if they hadn't so many mouths to feed. Four of his sisters were sent to convents on their fifth birthday, and he was given to the Benedictines as a small boy and raised within their walls, under their Rule. For the first month (he confesses, leaning in close enough she feels breath on cheek) he cried every night and begged each day to be allowed home. Several times he tried to escape. Once he made it as far as the township at the bottom of the great hill. He told anyone in earshot that he would never be a monk. He would be a warrior like his older brothers! He would head up King Louis' forces and take back Francia from the pretenders! He would he would he would, he shouted, as he was picked up by the back of his tunic and returned to the abbey.

She has never known a man to speak this way. She can see the weeping child in him. Is flooded with wonder that he has allowed her to.

The highest value of the Benedictines is humility, he tells her, of which obedience forms the core. The boy's *woulds* and *wills* were lectured, harangued, beaten out of him. The ideal is to have no desire other than to obey your masters. His masters were many; in the schoolroom, in prayer, in eating, sleeping, in all, he was observed. His head was always to be bowed, eyes downcast. He assumed always a phalanx of men watching him. It was safer that way. It was probably true.

'You become your own watcher,' he says. 'After a time, they need not do a thing, for you are always keeping guard over yourself.'

'How,' she asks him, her breath as short as though she's reached the highest branch of the old oak, 'did you become who you are?'

He considers the question. Tilts his head this way and that. Smiles. 'Who am I?'

'You . . . you are like a Roman soldier. No, don't laugh at me! I mean you are a—a part of a great army, yet also a person at ease with your place in the world. In command. You were a frightened child and now you are . . . you are you.'

'I could say the same of you, sister.'

Agnes swells with something she cannot name. She hadn't known she could be someone, become a person despite it all.

NOT A CONVERSATION FOR LADIES

UNUSUALLY, BROTHER RANDULF is among a company of men around the table. Agnes lingers as she serves, dares not join in as she would were the three of them alone.

For near a month a comet has lingered over Francian skies and talk of what it portends is the only talk in town. Her father tolerates it for one round of ale. 'Enough,' he says then. 'You sound like a mob of pagan peasants.'

'We are speaking as many in this good and godly place are,' Brother Randulf says.

Her father dismisses him with the flick of a wrist. 'You can witter on about portents day and night, and it will not change a thing on God's earth nor above it.'

Is the English Priest saying portents are not real? the gathered men want to know. Is it his view that God does not see fit to warn His people through such signs? Does he not believe the magi followed the Star of Bethlehem to the Christ child? Can he be so sure that this comet above is not a message like these others? How are we to know how to live, if not by the signs God sends us?

Brother Randulf cuts through the clamour: 'I am inclined to agree with the good English Priest, brothers. While it is true the Lord has on occasion communicated His will or warning through the heavens, those signs have been dazzling, insistent and accompanied by others of their kind. This lone, soft streak is like a red-skied morning or an uncommonly bright river flower: a reminder of the infinite variety of God's creation, but nothing more.'

Oh, Agnes thinks. You are a truly, truly brilliant man.

Thick and heavy silence, and she grows aware the men are looking at her where she stands behind her father's chair, ale jug in hand. Her father does not turn but his shoulders square, threateningly attentive.

'This is not a conversation for ladies,' he says.

Had she spoken aloud? The horror in some of these faces, amusement in others, tells her yes. She cannot bear to look at Brother Randulf before she flees to the kitchen. When she next sees him alone she will explain. As a child in the woods she would speak her thoughts to the frogs and birds, the piglets and grasshoppers. *Oh, you are a mischievous imp. Oh, you are a funny little beauty.* Just like this she has expressed her warmth and affection to him, her friend, Brother Randulf, forgetting such exuberance has no place in the adult world. He will understand, she is sure. He knows well the way her mind takes flight, knows she must sometimes bite down on her tongue so as not to exclaim her wonder and joy like a fool or a drunk. Like a child.

From the doorway, she listens as Brother Randulf continues. While he does not believe the comet is a portent, the people's panic must be taken seriously. He has seen, in his travels, a man burnt alive as a *tempestarius* after heavier than usual rain ruined already meagre crops. He has seen a woman's tongue cut from her mouth for calling forth a hail storm that destroyed the year's wheat one day before harvest.

'And I have seen worse than all that done to zealots who would not leave well enough alone,' her father says. 'So long as the people pray to the true God, we need not take their fairy stories from them as well. Our God is mighty enough to withstand the unintended insults of the foolish.'

The other men attempt to redirect the discussion to the possibility that this may indeed be a warning from God and that ignoring it is to condemn all people—superstitious or not—to pain and torment, but it is clear tonight is a contest between Brother Randulf and the English Priest, and before long the others are drawn onto its ground.

'It is true,' one says, 'that there is fear and blame afoot in town. They say this comet is our last warning and it must be heeded.'

'Indeed,' says another, 'there are those in this city have lived un-biblically for too long and the Lord will rain fire if it continues. So it is said.'

'I've heard nothing of the sort,' says another man. 'But, then, I so rarely consort with churls and fishwives.'

'I myself heard several such concerns in the market today,' Brother Randulf says. 'Kind Christian folk worried for the bodies and souls of certain sinners whose cloaks of piousness are known to be often discarded.'

There is accusation in his tone, though Agnes cannot determine its cause.

She creeps closer, sees that Brother Randulf and her father have eyes only for one another. The other men might as well have left hours ago so little do they matter in this room.

'It is late,' her father says, although it is not. He stands and the others do the same, gather cloaks and caps, leave quickly. One of the men leans into her father and whispers a few words before he goes. Her father stands still for a frighteningly long time.

—

The following day her father proclaims she is not to be alone in the company of Brother Randulf again. Not even on walks through the town. She has become far too familiar with him, and he with her. It is improper, and he, her father, is regretful he has not seen this earlier.

Agnes argues, and when that does not turn him she weeps, which only makes him surer. Such a womanly display of emotion is a clear sign that her regard for Randulf is not scholarly nor spiritual nor amicable. Nor could it ever be, as—and again her father takes full blame for not acting on this awareness earlier—she is no longer a child, and godly friendships between men and women are not possible.

Seeing he has worked himself into a priestly rage and that any further objection will result in a slap or worse, Agnes accepts his edict, says she will pray for forgiveness. She kneels by the bed in apparent supplication, makes a list in her head of all of the spiritually pure friendships between holy men and women. Paul and Thecla. Jerome and Paula. Of course, of course, Jesus and Martha too. Jesus and Mary. How could her father call these bonds ungodly? *He* is ungodly in his inability to understand *amicitia*. Ungodly in forgetting Christ's command to *Love each other as I have loved you.*

—

Her father leaves for the day, and within moments she has donned her cloak and boots. Righteousness is a wind at her back as she walks to the south edge of town then begins the climb to the abbey where Brother Randulf lodges. It is a clear, warm day, and from halfway up the hill she can see a trader boat approaching the Mainz port. From the top she sees far across the river to the old Roman arch at Kastel. Beyond that there are roads and woodlands she cannot name. She is struck by how much world there is around her and how little of it she knows.

Agnes turns her back on the view, the thought, and approaches the abbey. If the attending monk is surprised to see a lone woman at the gates he does not show it. He escorts her to a small courtyard with a stone bench, and bids her wait there while he fetches Brother Randulf.

Sweat drips from her neck into her tunic, from her forehead into her eyes. The climb was not so hard, but it is unseasonably hot and there is no breeze at all. Still, the courtyard is sheltered from the sun by the walls of the church and more peaceful than any place she has been.

Though I have barely been anywhere at all, she remembers.

Footsteps from a dark passageway and then there is Brother Randulf. He stops short on seeing her.

'You should not be here, Agnes. Your father—'

'My father is a fool.'

His face reddens and he moves towards her. 'The walls have ears. Hush yourself.' He nods at the gate she came through. 'We may walk a little.'

It is baking hot on the bare hillside, yet Randulf strides towards the river as though his blood needs heating.

'I am the fool,' he says, when they are some way from the abbey. 'I told the English Priest of gossip in town. I meant it as a stab at him. I should have foreseen he would turn his gaze on me. On you.'

'Brother, you must know I am innocent in my affections.'

He does not look at her. 'Your outburst last night suggests otherwise.'

'I was only—'

'It doesn't matter, Agnes. I cannot be near to you. Go home.'

He takes off forcefully through mud-thick river reeds and she struggles to keep up, her boots made heavier with each boggy step.

'Please stop,' she calls. 'Please, brother.'

He does, turns, still some distance away.

'You must know my love for you is of a sister for her brother. There is no reason for our friendship to end.'

He watches his feet as though they will run off without him. 'Your words last night stripped away a veil. Your father has seen what I have tried to deny.'

'No, no. It is only my undisciplined mouth! As a child, when the frog would leap just so and I would exclaim out loud—'

'I am no frog and you no child.'

'Brother, please, I—'

'I am no brother to you! Hear me, Agnes. I feel for you as a husband for his wife. That is what your father saw. You are not safe with me.'

It is as though he has thrown her across the back of a courser and slapped it with a switch of fire. It takes a long moment for her mind to catch up. By the time she protests that she feels as safe as a swaddled babe in arms, he has moved far ahead and she must run, her feet sinking deep with each step. When she reaches his side he turns on her in fury.

'Why will you not go? Oh, if you knew my thoughts you would flee!'

The crack in his voice! The wildness in his eyes! Oh, what thoughts they must be to create such a storm in him. *Tell me all*, she wants to say.

'You are too hard on yourself, brother,' she says instead. 'Even the sainted father of your order struggled with impure thoughts.'

He smiles unhappily. 'Would you have me roll in thorns and bramble, Agnes?'

An image from Benedict's *vita* comes to her: the venerated monk naked, pale skin lacerated and burred, face ravaged with pain. She has known the story most of her life, never once considered the why of it.

'Why did he do that, the thorns and bramble? Why not prayer and fasting?'

Randulf considers the question, as though they are back at her father's table discussing a point of canon law. 'When a person is consumed by physical torment it can be difficult to fully attend to spiritual tasks. Pain can be an intermediary salve.'

'Are you in torment, brother, truly?'

'Truly, yes.' He looks to the sky. 'For reasons only He knows, God has made you male of mind and heart, and female of form. Perhaps if I did not have such a base and sinful nature I would be able to enjoy the friendship and love of the man without wanting to lay with the woman.'

Mud seeps into her shoes and something like it clots her mind. Men at her father's table speak of this act as though it were as necessary as food or prayer. *This fool has acted the goat, but who can blame him when his wife is ill all the time? This lad must be found a wife before he falls on his poor old cow.* Benedict in the brambles and Randulf in torment and her own father betraying all to lay on her mother and nobody ever speaks about why. The beasts do it so there will be more beasts, but why, if not for that, are these men driven so?

'Why?' she asks. 'Why is it you want to lay with me?'

'For the love of God, Agnes! Do not ask me such things. I cannot speak of this with you.'

'Speak of it to the man in me. This great friend of your heart and mind. Tell him.'

He laughs, the sound tight and mean. 'And here is proof after all that no part of you is a man. A man as grown as you would not need to ask such things.'

'You are angry with me and I am sorry for that. I only want to understand what it is, this force that must tear through and wreck bodies and lives and friendships.'

'It is better to never know. How I wish I did not. Once you have felt what it is to—'

'But you are a monk!'

'I have been trying to tell you, Agnes, that I am in fact a man. I am a man who knows that when a man joins his body with a woman it is . . . Ah! It is . . . You want to know? Truly? It is as though I am a small child again running wild through the woods behind my parents' home and the harder I run the more I want to run. So I do, faster and harder and further, and then all at once there is a stream before me and I leap like a panting deer and plunge into the coolest, clearest, sweetest water, and it is like that even when I care nothing for the woman and the woman cares nothing for me. It is like that and, knowing this, I can't help thinking how much more it would be with a woman

I cherish better than any other soul on earth. To emerge from the stream and be held in the heated gaze of love.'

'Oh.'

A shiver passes through her, and when it is gone they are in near darkness. The preternaturally clear and bright sky has turned heavy and purple. The panicked cries of blackbirds flocking overhead is everything for a moment and then there is silence thick as a dungeon wall.

Randulf stares at her as though she conjured the change herself. 'Enough. Go home now.'

'I will not.'

'You must. Look how the sky darkens.'

The sky, my heart, my world. All growing dark too quickly, she thinks.

'I do not wish to go home. I wish to lay with you.'

'Oh, Lord. Agnes. No.' His head back in his hands.

The mud sucks at her feet as she moves closer, places her hands over his, draws them from his face. 'I wish to know what you know. I wish for you to show me.'

He looks at her in the eerie light and at once there is a heat in her that could boil the river dry.

'You don't know what you're saying. Go home. Go now.'

If she opens her mouth she will set him alight with her breath. Burn him to ashes where he stands.

If she stays silent she will combust like a hay store.

'I know well what I am saying, brother. Believe me on this.'

Faster than a hare he springs, brings her down into the reeds, lifts her skirt. Pain so searing she thinks something has gone terribly wrong, but soon it subsides and she is flat, full, stifled. His eyes are blurred as a drunk's; the grim, determined line of his mouth as strange and frightening as the light. He is running for that stream and she is the grass trampled beneath his feet. A sound like a man falling from a roof, a sudden lifting of the weight and then his violent shuddering into the mud.

'Agnes.' He is on his knees, weeping. 'You have—'

His words are stopped by an unearthly noise. Water erupts from the river and they stare at each other, shockingly, insensibly wet. The earth tilts, they tumble, cling together in the reeds as the purple sky swells like the sea, and branches and birds rain down.

IT HAS BEEN DONE BEFORE

IT SEEMS A capricious giant has passed through town, stamping one house into the dirt while leaving the next three standing, tossing a cart and both horses onto this roof here; over there, kicking a stone wall on top of a mother and her baby while the child toddling in front is untouched.

The house Agnes fled has crushed the father she disobeyed. Her neighbours whose homes were spared believe the quake came with purpose and achieved its aims. None of them say as much to her, the grieving and homeless daughter. They do not need to; the word all over town is that God has been merciful in sparing the just. Only a dozen dead and each a known sinner.

—

'For what sin was that infant known?' she rages to Randulf, who has left her side only to arrange her father's burial and her accommodation in the convent of Altmünster and to return to his own quarters for sleep and prayer. He was known to be a great friend of the English Priest and is of course a trusted brother of Fulda. There is no reason for anyone to look upon his care of Agnes with suspicion. She herself would not without the recent memory of him rutting her in the mud.

'We are all of us sinners,' he soothes, chastely distant in the convent garden. 'It is arrogance to claim to know God's mind in taking some and leaving others.'

'There are other punishments, besides.' She gestures to the dorter she is to call home. She gestures to herself, owning nothing but the clothes she wears, scrubbed of river mud and sweat by scowling nuns while she, wearing a borrowed novice's shift of the coarsest wool, wept for her father.

'I have arranged a meeting with the Archbishop two days from now. He loved your father and will want to assure your future as best he can.'

'I have no future.' Again she flicks her hand towards that grim hall. 'The most the Archbishop will do is convince the abbess to allow me to take orders. Make me an oblate rather than a charity case.'

'Your father had many friends. Perhaps . . .'

She knows the suggestion he struggles with and will not help him.

'There may be among them a man in need of a wife,' he says at last.

'If there was, he would have contracted with my father years ago. I am unmarriageable; it is a fact.'

His face reddens. 'Were I free to . . . I have thought of it, Agnes. I have. You know of Brother Gottschalk?'

She nods. There was much talk of him at her father's table some years ago. A child oblate of Fulda who, on reaching adulthood, took a case to the Archbishop of Mainz claiming it was illegal and immoral to force the vow on a child before he has the maturity to understand what it is he commits to. He won the fight, but his abbot appealed and the decision was overturned. Gottschalk was released from Fulda but not from monastic bond and lives now, presumably in misery, in Corbie.

'So you know it has been tried,' Randulf says. 'And by a man with great familial wealth and powerful friends. If I were to . . . I would lose. I would be more constrained than ever. Watched over constantly, no longer free to move in the world. Agnes, I have thought it through, believe me. If there was any way I could marry—'

'I am glad for it,' she says. 'I would dislike marriage very much. I've cooked and cleaned for my father enough to know taking care of a man is a thankless and endless drudge, and childbirth might as well be war for all those left dead and bloodied. As much as I dread the veil it is better than all that.'

He smiles, the first for days. 'There is nothing of marriage you would like?'

'I cannot think of a single thing,' she says, and his face returns to desolation. As is right.

In the days following her father's death Agnes refuses sustenance and sleep. All night she remains on her knees, praying for mercy. She sinned gravely and it is right she be punished. She does not pray, therefore, for a better life, only that she might stop desiring one. She asks God to take her rage and ambition, her selfish yearning for the life lost along with her father. She prays He will take away her wanting and leave only acceptance.

She prays and finds herself standing under a scorching sun, surrounded by pale stone walls. At her feet is a pile of bones she knows to be her own. There, her empty skull. There, her tiny heartless chest. Her sharp and childless hips. Her forever still limbs. Yellow dust swirls in the wind and blows clean through her unfeeling remains.

She wakes, and the urge to unlatch the door and flee into the night is stronger than any thirst or hunger she has known. From the quality of the dark she knows sleep has been brief. The first moments of sleeping are when the veil between worlds is thinnest. But demons and angels both may come at this time, and which of them brought her the vision she does not know.

In the garden the next morning she wants to tell Randulf of her dream, but he will not hear it.

'Divination of dreams is forbidden for good reason, Agnes. Even where the devil is not intervening it is too easy for a layman to read signs where there are none and to bend the meaning of the vision to confirm his own will.'

She fails to see how she can bend a vision towards her will when she has none. But it is clear Randulf is not in a mood to converse. He has received a message calling him back to Fulda. He must leave the next morning and does not know when he might return.

'The abbess will keep you until I can meet with the Archbishop to determine—'

'Take me with you to Fulda.'

Her will has made itself known after all, surprising her as much as Randulf, who laughs, says, 'Agnes!' Laughs, says, 'Agnes! What—Agnes!'

'You said yourself I have the mind of a man. Let me use it.'

Any reasonable person would assume she has lost her wits through grief and self-mortification. Randulf, though, considers her with the seriousness he has always shown her ideas. 'Your mind is quicker than any I've known. Your education has been eccentric and erratic, but no worse than that of others who come late in life to the abbey. Better than many.'

'It has been done before,' she reminds him, heart galloping to a lather. 'Thecla, Marguerite, Eugenia and others beside. All of them sainted in the end for their deceptions.'

He is quiet awhile. She closes her eyes, listens to the joyous trills of birds overhead. Is it their first song since the quake or is she reawakening to the world only now?

'It is not impossible,' Randulf says, and she opens her eyes, lets him see the hope within them. 'Your figure is straight enough. Your face and speech not overly womanly.' He is looking her over in the way of a trader assessing a sow rather than a man about to push his lover into the mud. 'The robe and cape make all of us formless and shadowed besides. Nevertheless, there is much risk. If you are detected you will be—'

'All I want from this life is to be allowed to read and pray and to contemplate the things I have learnt. A future that does not allow for this is no future at all. I would rather risk the fiercest shame and even death than resign myself to a life that is less than it might be.'

Ah, there is the look she'd seen on the riverbank before the world shook apart. If she is not more careful in expressing her passions she will be thrown on her back again. Indeed, after checking the surrounds he seizes her by the shoulders, says her name so it sounds like a prayer.

'Agnes, there is a happiness in my being I did not know possible. Days ago I was in despair at losing my greatest friend, yet here on the other side of disaster you have shown me the way to a miracle I did not have the imagination to pray for.' He squeezes her shoulders hard enough to lift her from the ground, laughs and releases her so he can catch her face in his burning hands. 'There is no risk I would not take to have you living by my side, both brother and wife.'

'Wife?'

'In all except law. In spirit and heart and flesh.' His face now pink and joyful; so different to the grim, red mask she saw when he was upon her in the mud.

'I thought I was clear, brother. I do not wish for a husband. Not in law or any other way.'

He steps back, regards her with an expression of great concern. 'I have heard the first instance can be a trial for a maid. Now that the perforation has occurred, perhaps—'

'I beg you to stop speaking of it.'

'I cannot. Our union only confirmed for me that—'

'I will offer myself as an anchoress if you do not stop.'

'Agnes. You would go mad before the mortar dried.'

'I will go mad if you will not stop talking to me of wife-ness or anything like it.'

A breath, eyes to the sky. 'So I must accept you are not your father's daughter in this respect, at least.'

The ground shakes. It is happening again. Perhaps this time she will be taken. She closes her eyes and waits. The moment passes and she still stands, still breathes. Randulf appears not to have noticed a thing.

'I do not mean to speak ill of the dead,' he says. 'You must know your father's weakness for flesh.'

She had not, though the moment Randulf says it she sees it is true. Tears slide from cheek to throat.

'It is not the worst of sins, whatever they'—he waves at the buildings beyond—'might tell you. Indeed, I've heard it said that even the great and pious Charles had urges so powerful he sometimes resorted to his unmarried daughters to salve them. At least your father—'

'Stop!' She heard this rumour at her father's table. A man who rarely visited spoke in praise of the great king, offering the uncontrollable urges as proof of his virility. He wondered aloud how heavily God weighed such sins against the ultimate heft of uniting half the known world under Christ. Surely, the man had said, King Charles has done more to earn his place in heaven than any man since Peter, but daughter-wounding is a serious thing, and so perhaps he must spend a few years with rats gnawing at his nethers in purgatory first.

The man had barely finished this sentence when her father punched him on the nose and told him to leave and never return.

'I have upset you,' Randulf says. 'I only wanted to—'

'Stop,' she repeats. 'I do not wish to lay with you again. Even if you talk at me for a thousand days, I will not. If that means you will not take me with you to Fulda then so be it.'

He looks at her with eyes like a kicked dog's. 'I am taking you to Fulda because that is where you belong, Agnes. Your willingness or not to lay with me has no bearing.'

She exhales, nods. 'Tell me what I must do to prepare.'

'I will find clothes to disguise you as we travel,' he says, the hurt sliding from his eyes and into his moving mouth. 'Meet me in the north barn after Lauds tomorrow. We will be clear of the town before you are missed at Prime.'

The dun-coloured tunic he has procured is shorter and tighter than her own and seems designed to draw attention to the breasts. Randulf regards her like a puzzle for a moment, then takes up her discarded long tunic and tears several wide bands from it. On his own chest he shows how she might bind herself and then turns to preserve her modesty as she does so.

'Better,' Randulf says in a tone that means terrible. He hands her a hooded cape, large enough to cover her twice, and though it stinks of horse sweat and old ale, it will do well enough for the journey.

At Fulda, she will don the voluminous robe of the Benedictines, which will easily disguise her form. With the hood draped low over her forehead and billowing out past her cheeks she will blend into the ranks of identically swathed figures.

'Your hair,' Randulf says, moving behind her and tugging her braid. She hears the rasp of a knife, winces as the braid hits the dirt. He works gently at her nape, his touch sure. She could be the hundredth girl in a row to have her hair lopped short by this man. The thousandth.

'Who cuts your hair, Randulf?'

'Brother Gerhold. He will do yours, too, when you are admitted. Tonsure you.'

She is almost as close to Randulf as when he pierced her in the mud. She imagines this Brother Gerhold pressed against her back just so, his hands brushing and smoothing her face and neck.

'Perhaps you could do it? I fear this other brother will know what I am.'

'That man couldn't tell an udder from a bullock sac if it was swinging in his face.' He steps away, moves around her. 'Fine job I have done,' he says, sorry and sad as if he's blackened her eye. 'You are a stranger.'

She kicks at the braid on the ground, breaking it into strands. Kicks dirt and old straw over the lot of it. The roof of this barn barely deserves the name; next rain, the ground will turn to sludge and her hair a part of it. If the birds or crawling insects or wind have not already taken it all. She thinks of her dream: her bare and lonely bones. The way it made her want to run until she burst through the skin of the world.

'We must start,' Randulf says.

She follows him from the barn, across the field and down to the river, walks through the reeds where they rutted and, without a word, they reach the bridge before the light has fully broken. Randulf hesitates as though waiting for a door to swing open and welcome him across. Agnes strides past him, does not turn to check he has followed. She is a tarnished maid with no father, husband, property or wealth. She is strong bones holding thick, firm flesh; a mind and soul that caused a brilliant monk to fall in love. There is nothing behind her and the whole of God's creation calling her from ahead.

HOPING FOR KINDER CONDITIONS

TO AVOID THE villages where the abbess may think to search for her missing orphan, they take the Antsanvia through the forest along the watersheds. Agnes has never been further from home than the great oak a morning's walk into the woods on the other side of the river. Her father said a girl planning to travel by road was like a fish planning to swim in a boiling pot. She asked why bandits, slavers and Northmen should be worse met for a girl than for a man. Her father said the worst that could happen to a man was he'd be killed. There were things done to girls that made them beg for the kindness of murder.

She repeats this to Randulf as they walk through the strange pale trees past Kastel in the stingy light of dawn. She is afraid and wishes to know of what.

'Your father will have seen many men beg for death. He knew well there are far worse things for all of us.'

'And are we likely to meet such things on this journey?'

'If we do they will find their own wish for death quickly granted.' Randulf plunges a hand into the folds of his robe, pulls out a knife the size of her forearm.

'Do you have one of those for me to carry?'

'I will be with you every step. Besides'—he tucks the knife away—'I have never met real trouble on this way. Bandits wait for the carts or watch the river. A couple of brothers with a sparse sack each might as well be invisible.'

The forest grows dark and cold as a fireless hall. The beeches grow in thick clusters, crowding out the other trees, their canopies spreading and blocking the sky. Some of these clusters have been here since before the Romans, Randulf says, and Agnes squats low, touches the mossy earth that has, perhaps, never known sunlight.

It may have known her father, she realises. He known it. This territory and further north still was his mission field. He knew the bursts of light leading from the end of one beech cluster to the next. Knew this slippery ground, these birds whose song is pot lids clanging. He never told her any of it. Not even the butterflies with white gossamer wings like the angels in her illustrated Scripture.

'My mother. Is this the way she would have come? In reverse, I mean?'

He shakes his head. 'Your parents will have travelled by boat. Gentler and faster. Better all round for those with the means.'

She tries to imagine her mother. A girl, younger by some years than Agnes is now, accompanied by an old man who was her husband. Did she know already she was with child? Was she excited by her future or frightened? Was it a relief or a horror to wake those first mornings in Mainz, a place so different that nothing could remind her of all she had lost?

They weave a boy out of air as they walk.

The closer her new story is to the true one, the simpler it will be to keep hold of. She will still be newly orphaned, educated for some years at home by a scholarly father. He cannot be a priest, of course. A scribe for the See, they decide, since there are dozens and none of them known outside of their work chambers.

'He must still be an Englishman,' Randulf says. 'As explanation for your oddities.'

'Do I have oddities?'

'For a man, many.' He smiles with the side of his mouth. 'Though fewer than you have as a girl.'

So, the story will go, this strange, highly educated boy left destitute by the father's death threw himself on the mercy of a passing Benedictine and, while begging for alms, quoted St Augustine on charity as a virtue that unites us to God. On questioning, Randulf discovered the boy was as proficient in Latin as any of the scholars at Fulda. He tested the boy's script and reading, his theological knowledge and spiritual commitment, and found him worthy of a place in their community. If, of course, the abbot thinks it should be so.

If they can convince the abbot to accept her she will rarely need to account for herself thereafter. The Benedictine Rule, which all within are bound to follow, forbids unnecessary talking.

'There are men I've lived with most of my life without knowing where they were born, who their fathers are. It is not done to exchange histories or probe for intimacies.'

'How then did you become so good at these things?'

'I am like Pliny's parrot. Ever wild, ever canny. I repeat the words of my master only so long as he is holding an iron bar and the key to my cage.'

'Have you decided on a name?' he asks when they are leaning against a great beech to eat a morsel of the black bread he has packed.

She tells him she will be named for her father and he smiles, tells her he only learnt her father's name at the burial service. 'He was always the English Priest, nothing else.'

'Not to me.'

After a while he says, 'Yes, good. You will be Brother Johann.'

'No. His true name. The name his mother gave him.'

'His English name?'

She nods.

'John.' Like a hoarse dog's bark.

'John,' she agrees, and from her mouth it is gruff and strange. The name of a man she knew her whole life; a name she has never spoken out loud. Old and brand-new and perfect for who she must be now.

They have been walking most of the day through forest, mud catching her feet, wanting to turn her ankles. Branches scratching her arms, biting insects on her hands and face. Relief to see now only cleared paddocks either side and firm packed earth beneath her boots. A moment only of this relief before she sees a mule coming their way, men walking either side and a few behind. At once this road is too open and clear. No bushes to hide behind, no trees to climb.

'Fellow travellers,' Randulf says with calm cheer, though she notices his right hand moves to the inner folds of his cloak.

The mule, the people, walk as though the dry road is knee-deep mud. Agnes and Randulf slow too. The mule's hooves strike the ground, and though Agnes has heard this sound her whole life, on this open road it thumps in her chest like a threat.

'Randulf.'

'All is well, Agnes. All is well.'

Close enough now to see the eyes of the travellers, weary and wary. Three men of middle years and a boy her own age level with the animal. A man as old as her father and a woman older still moving behind. Their clothing long since covered by road dust. Their faces and hands too. Like they've crawled out of their graves and not had time to wash. Even the mule appears dragged from the tallow pit and loaded with sagging, filth-covered sacks.

'Good day,' Randulf says.

Agnes stays a step behind, eyes focused on the ground, praying her hood conceals her face and that she will not be called on to speak.

'Good day,' says one of the men. 'We do not wish any trouble, sirs.'

'You will find none with us. We are Brothers of Fulda and go always in peace.'

'We wish you fair travels, brothers.'

The mule and its sorry keepers continue past.

'Harmless, as most are,' Randulf says when the mule's clop has faded.

'I should like to know why they are out here, travelling so harshly.'

'Hoping for kinder conditions, I suspect.'

'Is it so much colder in the north?'

'Colder and harder in other ways too. Not only the north. The further one goes from a Christian city the worse everything becomes.'

'Of course, without God—'

'It is not the absence of God that creates the hardship. It is the absence of churches and their coffers. The bigger the cathedral, the better the town's ale houses and merchants. Do you think Mainz thrives so because the people believe in God? It thrives because there are so many churchmen insisting on the finest cloths and meats and having the ready coin to pay for it.'

She thinks of her father's meticulous account ledgers, his chest bursting with coin. A gang of men from the See swept through and claimed it all before her father was even buried. Claimed, too, the silver candlesticks and goblets, the few dishes that survived the quake. The blankets and silks. Every one of the books. His wealth was his earthly reward for his services to the church; now he has gone to his final and greatest reward, the riches belong to those still toiling.

The need to relieve herself grows until she has no choice but to ask Randulf to wait as she squats between a close cluster of trees. It is quiet enough she can hear him pissing nearby and hot panic grips her.

'Randulf,' she says, when they are walking again, 'do the men of Fulda go as other men do? Out in the open, I mean.'

'Nine-tenths of the Rule is ensuring men of Fulda do *nothing* as other men do. We sleep in our clothes, wash rarely, and then alone and in haste. And as for the latrines, the block is divided into cells fit for an anchorite, lest a man catch even a glimpse of ankle as his brother raises his robe. Your modesty would not be better preserved were you empress of the realm.'

It is not her modesty she is concerned about but her very life. She cannot tell him so. He might take her lack of shame as provocation, her fear as unworthiness. He knows everything about Fulda, nothing about how it might be for her.

They stop for the night in a village barely worth the name. Four houses on one side of a dirt path, three on the other. Each appears no more than a single room. A scattering of pigs and chickens wander the place at will, and Randulf explains they're owned in community by the people here.

An ancient man with no hair and few teeth greets Randulf with a nod and leads them into his home. There, they sit on straw and drink thin soup as the last of the light fades. The man does not speak as they eat. He clears away the bowls, points them towards a blanket laid out near the fire. 'Haffa share,' he gums.

Her whole life, save the week since the earthquake, she has slept in a room with only her father and perhaps a nurse. Since she could walk she had a wide pallet, a thick, soft mattress and piles of blankets to herself. Now she must do with sleeping alongside Randulf on a patch of cleanish straw with one thin cover between two of them. The room is as cold as outside and stinks of mice. It matters not at all. She is exhausted by the day's walking, the week's sleeplessness. The grief and destruction. The upturning of all. After a brief contest with Randulf over the blanket, and several readjustments to ensure it covers them both despite their lying with a rope of clear air between them, she is instantly and deeply asleep.

'That old man,' she says the next morning, 'he believed me a boy. A brother, like you.'

'No challenge there. Doesn't see well, old Grupper.'

'Sees well enough to serve up soup without spillage. And he heard me speak and all. Still he thought me a boy.'

'No reason he wouldn't. I said you were and that is what he saw. Same as the folk on the road. People aren't seeking for things they don't know.'

The entire village is out to wish them good travels. Thirty or so pairs of eyes watching the familiar monk and his new recruit. A girl her own age stops them with a gift of wrapped cheese; her mother asks if they'll say a blessing for the soul of her husband just passed. A man with a squealing piglet in his arms wants news from town, and as Randulf talks of politics and business, others gather and ask questions and sometimes Agnes answers, and when they finally are able to leave people say, *See you again, Brother Randulf, best of luck to you, young John.*

Her legs ache as though she's not rested them ever and new blisters bloom with every step. Still, she walks taller and with ever greater ease. What a thing it is to stand and speak to a person and have them not see you. To drop your hood and raise your face to the bright new day and still remain a secret.

That afternoon the rain comes hard before they reach the next village and they run for a cave. Randulf notices her shivering, insists she wear his cloak as well as her own. As he hands it to her there is just enough light to see the image of the Virgin stitched into the hood. She runs her fingers over it and Randulf tells her it is sewn into all the brothers' cloaks as protection against evil thoughts.

'And lice,' he adds.

Randulf builds a fire and they eat the rest of the morning's cheese with some hard bread. He takes a position closest to the cave mouth, further from the fire, falls asleep as soon as he is flat. Agnes shivers and rubs her bleeding feet. She has never built nor tended a fire without a hearth, and within the hour

Randulf's blaze is nothing but warm sticks and ash. She will never be able to sleep here in the cold, with not even the thinnest layer of straw to soften the stone. Defiantly she remains seated, glaring at the failed fire, and at dawn is woken by Randulf teasing her for having rolled in ashes while she slept.

The third and final night they stop in a guesthouse for pilgrims. As men of Fulda they are given the pallet closest to the fire and, though they must share it, they at least have a blanket each. Agnes sleeps in bursts between the huff of Randulf's breath on her neck, the crunch of old straw beneath, the snores and mutterings of a dozen strangers.

In the morning, the landlady brings Randulf a bowl of water, a sliver of soap and a small piece of mirrored glass to prop against the wall. 'I always shave before I leave here,' he explains, soaping over the sparse hair that has appeared on his cheeks and chin these last days. 'In the abbey we are only allowed the luxury twice each month.'

A new panic. 'All the brothers will be half-bearded save me! I will be found out.'

Randulf, calm and easy as ever, edging the blade across his jaw. 'Not all men grow beards so quickly. Many are near as smooth-cheeked as girls the whole month long. Indeed, some say it is a sign of great holiness. A blessed lack of carnality.'

'So I am safe?' she asks.

'Entirely,' he says, and is that a melancholy sigh or an exhalation of pleasure as he presses the warmed cloth to his naked face?

Late that morning the abbey appears high on the hill, its stone asserting authority over the scattered wood huts of Fulda village below. It has the air of an ancient Roman temple although it is barely even old, the very first of its edifices constructed in 744. She knows the date from Boniface's *vita*, knows too that the saint's bones lie in the church and that countless miracles have been realised by those who make the pilgrimage to pray over them.

Not yet a hundred years and the abbey has grown from seven monks to more than six hundred, not counting the novices and children. Only a third or so live permanently here in the mother convent. Randulf assures her she will be one of them.

They pass through the village that serves the monastery. At a washing tub in front of a long hall there is a girl of Agnes's age, huge with child, a babe and a small boy sleeping at her feet. Two younger girls sit nearby, cloth across their laps, needles in their hands. An older woman approaches, says something that makes the mother break into a great, shining smile. The older woman whoops with laughter, lowers herself to the ground, catches up the babe and swings it gently. One of the younger girls presses her hand to the cheek of the other, who leans her head towards her sister just so. The elder begins to sing and the others join in.

Agnes does not recognise the language, but the tune is sweet and cheer-filled and it washes her through with grief. It might have been nice, after all, to have had a mother to braid her hair and wash her face and worry that she spent too much time reading and not enough learning to weave or pickle. A mother to teach her how to be one herself. To want to be.

Agnes watches the women in their work circle. She could still turn off this path. Too late to be mothered, but not, perhaps, too late for sisterhood. She could follow the example of St Radegund, take her learning to a convent and forward the cause of other women. She could scribe and interpret. Read and teach. Copy manuscripts to procure wealth. Be of service to her sisters instead of exiling herself from them forever.

'The folk here are all Christians,' says Randulf, 'though they sometimes sing pagan songs.'

'And who can judge them, when the song is so very pretty?'

'Many in your new home judge them harshly indeed. You'll do better to pretend you agree.'

'What's one more pretence?' she says as they leave the women and their song behind and begin the climb to the abbey. The truth is she has never been part of that world. It would be folly to attempt to enter it—and so wholly!—at this advanced age and with the knowledge of Latin, politics and the cold carnality of men already within her.

DRESSED IN THE CLOTHES OF A MAN BY A CERTAIN LOVER OF HERS

(836-841)

ORA ET LABORA

SHE HAS NEVER known tiredness like that of her first months at the abbey. Her narrow pallet is one of dozens in a dorter so vast that the furthest are not visible from the doorway. Every pallet occupied by a monk who is also a man and therefore prone to all the snores, farts, sleep talk and night moans as any other. High windows run the length on both sides, letting in sweet air but also vicious cold and so the shutters are often closed and, sometimes, brothers stuff cloth into the gaps in a feeble attempt to block out the chill. All night a lamp burns and the circator makes regular checks to ensure no man removes so much as a cord from his clothing or rises before the bells. Her robes itch and the bindings press deep into her flesh, but terror of discovery is stronger than discomfort and so she lies still as a fallen log.

Miserable though it is in bed, she wishes for more time there. To lie with eyes closed if not actually to sleep. The Divine Office more demanding, more disrespecting of rest than a newborn infant. Bells rouse them at the darkest hour for Nocturnes, and they must traipse down the night stairs to kneel on the packed earth floor, the smell of unwashed men pulled from never-clean beds and irritating flicker of candles the only things stopping her from sinking back into sleep. Afterwards only the barest couple of hours to rest before being roused to sing Lauds. Then every few hours the bells calling her back to the cold, stinking church for Prime, Terce, Sext, Nones. Every day at least one additional mass and sometimes two. Several days a week they sing Psalms for the deceased. Always, Vespers as the sun goes down and, finally, in the full darkness of night, Compline.

Between Prime and Terce they gather in the chapter house and listen as a brother reads from the Rule. Morning after morning, chapter after chapter, starting over again when done and onwards like this forever more. Day after day after day after day they are reminded that they must be content with the meanest and worst of everything, call themselves the lowest of the low, take no independent action. It is a revelation that these men struggle and need constant correcting in order to live as women must.

After the reading of the Rule, there are announcements about the business of the place and then it is time for the brothers to hear each other confess and seek penance (as though sitting on bare stone for the hour is not punishment enough). Certain among the brothers are eager to confess the most minor sins and beg the harshest punishments. The abbot is most generous in his willingness to let those who long to scourge their flesh or kneel on nettles do so frequently.

After confessions come accusations. It is good for your brother's soul to speak of his sins if he cannot or will not. Perhaps. More often it is done to assuage a petty vendetta or out of simple dislike. Even when the error reported is severe, such as when a brother assisting the cellarer is accused of having taken for himself provisions meant for the destitute, there is a visible pleasure in certain of the assembled company when the guilty man is hauled onto the tiles to have his bared buttocks whipped until he faints.

She takes careful note of those whose faces flush at the bloodied welts and pained gasping. Flush in the way of one not enraged but engorged. She fears these men as anyone would fear a beast who hunts out of lust rather than hunger, but no more than she fears the brethren who report on others out of genuine concern for their souls. She fears every man in the place save the one who brought her. Any of the others might, out of holy intent or wicked, report her for an infraction, and the moment her robes are lifted to the whip her life will be done.

She wards off the terror with scrupulous obedience. If Benedict himself were watching from above he would call her an exemplar of all he intended. She is ever aware, though, that the true threat is her body. The robe and cowl cloak her in anonymous maleness, but multiple times a day, in the dim and fetid privacy of the latrine, she checks and rechecks the firmness of her bindings.

In the voices of her brothers she hears every variation of depth, but still she worries her own will betray her. She works on it during the endless singing; learning the way her chest and throat feel when she matches, as one is supposed to in chant, the tones of the men around her.

Most of all she dreads the monthly blood, keeps her pockets filled with moss and leaves, an extra strip of linen. But when it comes it is barely noticeable—lightened, perhaps, by the lack of meat and excess of labour. Or perhaps God has eased her curse. Perhaps it is His way of showing He approves.

She had thought the long periods of enforced silence would be difficult, but as she gets to know her brothers through gesture and action, through confession and accusation, she sees there are few she would wish to speak with if she could. She had thought the restriction on laughter would be difficult, too, but nobody jokes, and although there is much absurdity it is the kind that makes one want to write a treatise rather than laugh out loud.

Mealtime, for instance. Once a day in the cold months, twice on the longer, warmer days, they gather in the refectory. A senior brother is assigned reader and his voice drones (always, whoever it is, he drones) while the men eat silently and conduct what at first seem complex, important conversations using their hands. Time and experience prove that most of this gesturing and whirling, finger shaping and air poking is to say *pass the bread* and *the broth is salty* and *listen to how he drones*, and she longs to make the hand shapes she learnt in Mainz market: the ones the merchants and wives used to tell customers what they thought of their offer without wasting a breath.

Randulf is always there but so is everyone else. There is no privacy, no tolerance for particular friendships. She sees him every day, sleeps in the same hall every night, yet they rarely speak. Day by day, the flesh memory of him grinding her into the mud recedes and her craving for his company, for the long, winding conversations they once shared as they walked bareheaded around Mainz, rises.

When they are not praying or confessing or attempting to sleep they are working. Manual labour for two hours a day in one of the gardens or crop fields or with the horses, sheep or chickens. Most days it is bone-achingly cold, and as a city-bred novice her task is always either digging or shovelling.

At least outside the stench of men is diffused, the cloying incense and tallow stink almost forgotten. It is a blessing indeed to be allowed for two short hours to breathe instead cow dung and soil and pine, sweet wood smoke drifting from the kitchens, malty hops from the brewhouse.

Outside, too, her ears are spared the constant swish of cloister whispers, the drone—Lord forgive me—of Latin chants sung by rote rather than intention. Outside, it is spade meeting dirt, axe striking wood, pump handle squealing, water hitting stone, and every now and then a scrap of laughter drifts across the grounds and renews her hope that there is, in this place, at least one soul not exhausted into joylessness.

The rest of the work day is spent on tasks assigned to each brother according to his talents. It must be a hard thing, indeed, to be deemed naturally attuned to cleaning latrines and shovelling horse shit. There is no risk of this for her, a brother who can read several languages and write in two, in a community of which more than half are effectively illiterate. Still, she is not allowed to take up her assigned work until she has completed her noviciate, and so for this first year at Fulda she, like the other novices, is rotated through tasks under each of the obedientiaries and sub-obedientiaries: the cellarer, the kitchener, the *granatarius*, the guest master, the refecteror, the gardener, the *camerarius*, the sacrist, the *matricularius* and, most dreaded for the foul work as well as the foul temper of the man himself, the infirmarian.

Working alongside boys from the most famous noble families in Francia she is ever aware that—even with her particular skills, of which the abbey is in great need—it is only the special relationship Randulf enjoys with Abbot Hrabanus Maurus that allows her, a penniless orphan with no official education or connections, a place here.

Barely in his forties, with thick, wavy hair as black as befits a man named for a raven, Hrabanus is famous throughout Christendom as a leader and scholar. A child of Mainz, like her, he studied at the feet of Alcuin and was several times in the presence of Charles the Great. It is said he has travelled to every known country on earth and is fluent in every living language and some that are no longer spoken. He is expert in astrology, botany and theology as well as canon law. He was once Randulf's schoolmaster and has long been his mentor, and in hearing the abbot speak she often recognises not only the ideas but the precise way of phrasing them. She experiences the heavy thud of disappointment on realising that the man who dazzled her with his mind might have been merely stating things told him by another.

She wonders if the abbot himself is doing the same, if every man in the whole tall tower of brilliant men is taking from the one above and restating with the confidence of an originator. She wonders how a person might tell the difference between something that is true and something that has merely been repeated so often and for so long that it is carved into men's thinking like a desire path through the forest.

It is a hard, lonely, exhausting life, and if she could think of a place to run to where she would not be destitute or veiled, she would go at once. In the spare few breaths a day in which she can pray her own mind she asks God for a sign; He sends nothing but more bells to interrupt her sleep, more chants to practise, more dirt to shovel, more droning old men to listen to.

Nine months of this before she finds herself drifting to sleep with the thought that the mass of bodies in the dormitory is a single softly heaving animal whose presence soothes without demand. She wakes easily for Lauds, floats to chapel as if carried by the same gentle creature that blessed her sleep. Singing the office, she notices hers is no longer one voice straining to meet the others but a drop of water in a mighty sea. She is nothing and immense all at once.

In the hot, bright morning, chopping wood for the stores, she feels a new lightness in the axe, as though the arms of her brothers are joined in the effort. There is a sweetness to the scent of split beech as though the sacrificed tree is sanctifying her work. A cooling breeze kisses her face and she feels God in it. She is exactly where she should be and He, as always, is there too.

After twelve months, on the Feast of Perpetua and Felicity, she is brought before the whole community and the Rule is read to her in full, as it had been after two months and again after six. As on those occasions she is told, *This is the law under which you are choosing to serve. If you can keep it, come in. If not, you may leave.* This is the last time the offer will be made. If the young brother agrees to live by the Rule today, he is no longer free to shake its yoke from his neck.

She does not have a word for this feeling. Knowing she is an imposter, false and wicked, that a person so skilled at deception could never hear God's truth. Knowing equally that it is God who has placed her here.

Tremors in her hand as she signs her false name to a document promising stability, fidelity and obedience. She is not afraid, in this moment, of the hundreds of robed men crowded into the chapel, every one of whom (for Randulf is away on a procurement mission) would happily bury her in the latrine pit if they knew her true form. It is God alone she fears as she signs the parchment then places it on the altar, as she says, *Receive me, Lord, as you have promised, and I shall live.* She waits for the reliquary to combust, for the vaulted roof to crumble, for her eyes to turn inwards and her mouth fill with blood. The brothers of Fulda repeat her verse three times, add, *Glory be to the Father*, and so she continues the ritual, prostrating herself at the feet of the abbot and the obedientiaries and then the community as a whole, asking for their prayers.

The ground remains solid stone and the lamps do not so much as flicker and at the end she stands and Abbot Hrabanus places the monastic scapula over her head and not a single voice, let alone all of God's creation, rises up in protest.

LECTIO DIVINA

FATHER HATTO, THE *custos librorum*, who has spent years turning Fulda into the premier centre of learning in the empire, has heard about the young brother who reads Greek as well as Latin and is eager for him to begin work now he is avowed. There are tottering piles of manuscripts, scrolls and books from around the world (many, she knows, purchased by Randulf) which, due to lack of capable men, gather dust along the library walls. Brother John is to catalogue and shelve them.

The task is both easy and deeply pleasurable. Hatto—smaller than her, with a soft, motherly voice and a face webbed with creases—encourages her to stay and read whatever she likes in those precious few hours between Sext and Nones when the brothers are supposed to rest in silence. So it is in the sweet, warm June afternoons she reads *Noctes Atticae* and burns with frustration at being unable to comprehend the discussions of grammar. She asks Hatto what she can read to understand better, and he wanders away without answering, returning within the hour to place a tall stack of books at her knee.

She picks up Isidore of Seville's *Etymologiae*, which she is sure she has read multiple times in her father's house, and is mortified to find the text is ten times the length of the version she held dear. She reads it now and swells with questions her father will never be able to answer about why he gave her the books he did and what he thought he was making of her, a girl too educated to be content as a wife, yet too ignorant to protect herself from the world she thought she understood.

She gulps Boethius's *Consolation* like a thirsty horse at a stream, and although Hatto beams delightedly at her as she exclaims over the aptness of the image of fortune's wheel, he does not ask questions to help her think further, as Randulf would, and after a few such outbursts gently reminds her that reading time is to be silent.

On the Feast of the Beheading of John the Baptist, when the sun is so bright and hot it is easy to imagine herself in Galilee, she reads St Jerome's letter to Eustochium, a girl of thirteen. The venerated Christian elder warns the girl against the horrors of marriage and childbirth, tells her she should avoid consorting with married women in case they recruit her to their cursed ranks. *As long as woman is for birth and children*, he writes, *she is different from men as body is from the soul. But when she wishes to serve Christ more than the world, she will cease to be a woman and will be called a man.* The way to reach this blessed state is to *read often, learn all that you can. Let sleep overcome you, the scroll still in your hands; when your head falls, let it be on the sacred page.*

What an interesting thing, she thinks, that of all the books my father put before me he never brought me this one that is, after all, from a Christian elder and specifically and forcefully aimed at a curious girl such as I was. What a very, very interesting thing.

She reads Ambrose's assertion that there is no one way to worship God correctly, that in Rome one should worship the Roman way and in Milan as the Milanese do. She thinks of Randulf wolfing tranche after tranche of pork at her father's table, longs to ask him if Ambrose is how he justifies straying from the Rule when he travels and whether there are limits to how much one may conform to local ways.

She thinks again of her father and his stories of conquering pagans by allowing them to keep their own customs so long as they call them by Christian names. What's the point of it all—the liturgies and the psalms and the masses, the fasts and festivals and sacraments—if one can do them or not, at this time or that one, and still have entry to heaven? She calls to Hatto to ask, but he presses fingers to lips and continues his own reading.

As the afternoons cool and the air becomes loud with the harvests she develops an itch more powerful than the one caused by her robe and bindings. The physical irritation a lone flea that lands and doesn't bite compared to the vicious swarm of questions infesting her mind.

On Marymas, when the bell rings for Vespers, she does as always and follows Hatto down the library steps and across the grass to reach the chapel. The trees are barer than they should be this early in the season, though how would she know, having only spent one autumn in Fulda and that mostly in service of the *granatarius* and with barely time to notice if it were day or night.

Hatto shivers beside her. 'We shall be needing our winter cloaks early this year,' he murmurs. It is a rare thing for the man to speak and she will take it as an invitation whether it is meant so or not.

'Father Hatto, I am troubled,' she begins, keeping her voice and pace steady. 'There is much in the texts we collect that contradicts the Rule.'

'Brother,' he says, 'we read the ancients to understand the earthly realm, not the way of Christ, whom those unfortunates did not know.'

'Indeed, Father, yet I speak not of the ancients but of the church fathers. Augustine, Boethius, Jerome, Origen, Irenaeus, Tertullian.'

'You must return to the Scriptures, child. The church fathers were visionary and wise, but still only men. The Scriptures are the infallible word of the Lord, and in them we find the true way.'

'Forgive me, Father, but is it not true that—'

'Brother John'—Hatto stops, raises a hand to indicate she should do the same—'I urge you to return especially to Corinthians. St Paul's warning: *Let no man deceive himself. If any man among you seemeth to be wise in this world, let him become a fool, that he may be wise.*'

'It is because I wish not to deceive myself that I question these things, Father. I—'

'This is insolence, Brother John. Insolence and pride, antithetical to godliness. Anathema to monastic life!' Hatto's hood has been agitated half down his skull. The pale hair adorning his forehead is damp and wispy, as though he has been working at the forge. 'You will confess and seek penance in Chapter or I will be forced to do so for you.'

'Yes, Father.'

He nods and strides ahead. The bells ring and ring, and if she does not get to Vespers her punishment will be worse still. Insolence, yes. It is true. To think she knew this place and that man, her beloved librarian, well enough to speak to him as though he were Randulf or even her father. Pride, though: she cannot feel the truth of that. Does God not want us to use our gifts, which are, after all, from Him?

Her brothers file into chapel, this glorious flock of identical crows. Surely they each continue to live as selves despite their external sameness? Surely each man holds thoughts and passions and secrets within his robes. Secrets from each other but never from God. She realises she has assumed this. Insolence again. That she understood what it was to be a brother here. That it meant to live as she and Randulf do. Hatto has shown the error of this. To be a true monk one must abandon one's self entirely. Become not a man who conforms to the Rule but an indistinct part of a body that moves in the Rule without thinking.

It is difficult in this moment not to run.

In Chapter the next morning she stands to confess. Bowed black heads watch her without raising their eyes. One of them Randulf, one of them Hatto. She confesses insolence and pride, is relieved the abbot does not ask for details, does not require her to provide evidence. After a pause in which her thighs twitch and her mind maps the route to the forest, Hrabanus orders her to take meals alone after the rest of the community has eaten, for five days.

Oh, it is pleasant indeed to eat without the drone of the daily reader and the dry chafe of fingers signing pointlessly. On the second and fourth days Randulf strolls past the refectory as she eats, meets her eyes and spares her a small smile and so, in the end, the punishment brings her relief and happiness, and though she worries this is bad for her soul, which after all is supposed to be in penance, she does not confess lest this new sin bring a worse punishment, or a better one, to put her further into debt with the Lord.

Father Hatto was right, though, to send her back to the Scriptures. *Lectio Divina* is not reading like a starved dog eats, but allowing God to speak through His living word. She sits long hours with the Scriptures, does not fight their meaning or attempt to prove it one way or another.

O Lord, You have searched me and known me, she reads.

Even the darkness is not dark to You.

For You formed my inmost being. You knit me together in my mother's womb. I praise You, for I am fearfully and wonderfully made.

I am fearfully and wonderfully made, she reads and prays and feels and breathes and knows.

OPUS DEI

SHE ARRIVES AT the library as usual and Hatto signs *follow me*, leads her up the almost hidden stairs in the back corner of the room and into the fabled scriptorium. Perhaps he remains angry and wishes her gone from his daily sight, or perhaps it is a generous act of forgiveness. Perhaps it is merely that the demands on Fulda to produce more manuscripts for sale are great and a brother with the ability to write well cannot be wasted in cataloguing.

There are so many windows on the west and north walls, the room feels less like a room and more like a platform looking out over the abbot's house on one side and the church on the other. Under each window a slanted desk, and on a stool in front of each desk, a monk. Twelve in all, she counts, before the head scribe, Father Ermo, directs her attention to the large table in the centre of the room, upon which are spread a number of pages with glistening silver and gold decoration. Past it, along the inner wall, is a long bench where newly stretched and scraped parchment is being cut, pricked and ruled in readiness for the scribes. Over the bench, an inscription from Cassiodorus: *With his fingers he gives life to men, and arms against the wiles of the devil.*

Before she is allowed a desk she must learn the base trades, and so she is transferred to a workshop in the yard behind the refectory to spend her work hours soaking goat skins in lime-water, scraping away bristles and slivers of flesh, rinsing away the lime and stretching the skin on a rack three times as wide as her arm span before scraping it again, stretching it some more, scrape, stretch, scrape the drying skin for days. The closer the hides come to readiness, the more they resemble the skin of St Bartholomew hanging pale and loose in the moments after his flaying.

Her first attempts result in thick, yellowed sheets fit only for account-keeping, but under the tutelage of the parchmenter, a tall, long-fingered layman who calls her Holy Brother and begs forgiveness every time he must correct her, she learns to make pages smooth and translucent as shaved bone.

She is moved to the ink workshop, where she crushes oak galls into powder, blends the powder with rainwater and vinegar, later stirs in copperas and ground gum. The space is narrow and dark, the overseer a monk who refuses to speak and is quick with the switch if she fails to understand his gestures. Her hands, chafed by weeks of handling parchment, stain brown and purplish black where the ink soaks into open welts.

And all this time, nights spent studying by candlelight: the Tironian system of dots and dashes of the clerks, then the distinctive Fulda script which marks this abbey's manuscripts as authentic and therefore valuable. She practises on a wax tablet which Ermo inspects each morning, pointing out her errors, demanding she scrape it clean and begin again. It is months before she's allowed a meagre allowance of ink and a stack of parchment offcuts for her practice.

Even after she is admitted to the scriptorium proper, her apprenticeship is not finished. Here, for weeks that feel like years, she works alone at the bench facing the dark inner wall, cutting the parchment sheets to proper size, pricking and ruling them in readiness for words.

At the beginning of each work day, before the silence falls, Ermo reminds them that the texts they labour over will make their way to the richest chambers and the darkest corners of the known world. The books copied at Fulda command prices three times higher than those of any other house. Without our work, the entire order would eat nothing but leek soup year in and out, he tells them. So much for the rule of humility, she thinks.

Soon she understands that Ermo is only attempting to keep his workers from throwing themselves out of the windows or swallowing vials of viscous ink. The work is done for as long as daylight allows but, as everywhere here, only ever for three hours at a time, that being the maximum between prayer. Three hours of scribing feels to her back like a week swinging a hoe. No candles, lamps and certainly no fire is allowed (the story of the fire that destroyed the Library of Celsus centuries ago is relayed here as if it were witnessed last week by half the monks of Fulda) and so the same enormous windows that give them the light needed for work also make the room the coldest in all of the abbey. Perhaps the coldest place in all of the world, she thinks as she sits on her hands, shoves them inside her robes in between lines. She detests the scriptorium as much as she loves the library. She asks to be transferred, but there are so few with her knowledge of language and delicacy of stroke it is unthinkable.

A year passes, two. Ermo notices his most promising young scribe has the hunch of Pepin the Firstborn and orders a daily stride around the grounds immediately after Sext. For an hour a day she is ten again, running wild in the woods, though the trees are fewer and she dare not climb any of them, lest her privilege be revoked. Still, there are clusters of bright green grass amid blankets of pale hairy sedge. There is the river for which the monastery is named, and though it is not as grand as the Rhine, after rain its rushing sounds like her childhood. There are places dark as the night and those where the sun enters in a single beam, as if from God's finger. There are woodpeckers that appear to have dipped their heads into a vat of red lead meant for the illuminator's ink pot and whistling chats that swoop low enough that their wingtips kiss her hood.

She no longer needs the forest to feel close to God. Monastic life keeps Him near to her at all times. Still, she has missed witnessing so directly the wonder of creation. Easy to forget in the cloister how utterly, heart-swellingly beautiful is His world.

When the snow comes she replaces her walks in the woods with wandering the crypts below the abbey church. Here are the lesser relics of lesser saints: a strip of cloth someone pressed onto the tomb of a saint without a *vita*; a vial of oil dripped from a lamp burning near the grave of a long-forgotten minor bishop; a satchel of dust that may once have been a third-century martyr's hair.

But also, in the *tituli* written by Hrabanus back when he was a lowly schoolmaster, the story of how a desert cult became a mighty empire. In the eastern crypt are honoured the Hermetics in the desert and ascetics in the Holy Land, the slain children of Bethlehem and St George, the Roman soldier beheaded by Diocletian. In the western crypt are honoured the apostles and the missionaries, the coenobitical fathers of their own tradition. And crowded together with Genevieve, Scholastica and Brigid is an altar to her own, now secret namesake.

Agnes, a child of twelve, dragged through the streets of Rome for declaring Jesus her only and forever spouse. Thrown into a brothel where men were invited to rape Christ's young bride. Man after man struck blind before he could defile her. Enraged, her persecutors dragged her into the street and stripped her clothes but her hair grew instantly to cover her nakedness. They tied her to a stake in the centre of an arena and set the sticks beneath her alight. The fire burnt bright and high, devoured every scrap of wood as well as the ropes that held her so that, unburnt, she could walk away. Of course they did not let her; they came at her then with swords and stabbed and chopped and her blood came in such quantities and with such force that it filled the arena and drowned her murderers, flowed into the street where the Christians who mourned her soaked it up with cloths which they carried to every corner of Christendom.

So it is that, more than five centuries later, Agnes of Mainz can kneel in front of a stone altar that holds the blood of this tortured and murdered child. The altar is new enough, ignored enough, that when she kisses it tiny grains of stone dust stick to her lips. How many centuries will it take, she wonders, for hands to rub this slab as smooth and shiny as that of Benedict or Sturmi or any of the others that pilgrims flock to for cures, marriages, babies, rain? She will not live long enough to see it, she knows. Only a miracle—a big one, like a limb regrown or a crone swollen with child—would bring the crowds to Agnes's corner. Why reflect on the suffering of a little girl when there are dragon slayers and war heroes and steely ascetics to admire?

The pilgrims return with the warm weather and she again spends her free hour outside. On the Feast of St Barnabas she comes across a grove, hidden from the main path through the beech forest. The falling light catches in the overhead branches and she remembers the wood sprites she conjured in Mainz, moves towards the dancing light.

A grunt and she is all terror. This is not boar country, she knows, yet her body is seized with the certainty of tusks charging. There is no stench of pig here, though and—still—frozen—listening—it is clear this grunting is human. Her breath returns and she leans, does not dare step, towards the sound.

A brother with his back to a tree, closed eyes directed heavenwards, robes raised, partially covering the monk kneeling at his feet, suckling his member like a babe at breast.

She moves away as quietly as she is able. Her heartbeat is all wrong, takes effort to restore to rights. She understands now a genre of stories told at her father's table: stories of monks offering and taking unspecified indulgences to and from each other. A glimpse into a grove and a set of words she'd thought had one meaning are revealed to describe another set of behaviours entirely.

She is not innocent of carnality, yet the vision confuses and disturbs her. She bristles with questions.

Is this act known only to monks, or do farmers and artisans and merchants kneel in front of their fellows in this way? She sees the men around her father's table, one by one taking their place where she used to hide and hungrily unbuttoning their neighbour's breeches.

Do the men take turns to give and receive these ministrations? Could there be, perhaps, pleasure for the one attending as well as for the one attended to?

She remembers the forceful fit of Randulf's rod, wonders if it might have been better placed inside her mouth. If there might not be a certain enjoyment in learning its length with strokes of her tongue.

She wonders why thinking of this makes the place between her legs ache like she has ridden all day. Why it makes her want to straddle any passing beast and ride longer yet.

CLAUSTRUM

IN THE SPRING and summer months Randulf is often absent. She watches for new boxes of manuscripts to appear in the library, strains to hear the murmurings of Hatto and Ermo as they determine what is to be copied and how and for whom. Yearns for a mention of the brother responsible for the acquisitions, for word of his whereabouts and wellbeing, though such word never finds her ears.

Then each time her longing has been worn small and sharp as her nib, she will turn onto the night stairs or step into the library or cloister and there he is, eyes as bright with pleasure and promise as at her father's table.

Still there is little chance for them to speak. There is a nod and sometimes a small smile when he sees her across the dorter or in Chapter. Several times he has signed to her in the refectory: *Is all well with you, brother*? and she has replied, *It is. And with you?* and he has nodded and returned to his pottage. There have been short exchanges of news while passing in the yard here and there: her reporting on her work; him listing the cities he has travelled to lately, the texts he has purchased. Every time she wants to say: May we not speak as we used to? May we not be friends now we are brothers? She wants to say, Brother, I wait for you as the thirsty fields for rain.

Early autumn, her fifth year at Fulda, after one of these long, yearning absences, she sees him in the refectory. His face and hands, revealed in the act of eating, are as pale as at the end of winter. This time she finds in herself determination in place of helpless thirst. She will speak with him and at length, and she will do so without secrecy or shame. After all, Brother John, respected scribe, trained by Hatto and one of the few workers Ermo addresses by name and stops to observe for long moments on his way through the scriptorium, has every reason to consult Brother Randulf, the man responsible for procuring the abbey's most valuable manuscripts. Indeed, it is absurd they have not conversed regularly all this time.

The bell rings, all wipe their hands, replace their cowls, file silently from the refectory. She walks directly to him, murmurs (as is appropriate) but does not whisper: 'Brother Randulf,

I seek your guidance on the texts recently brought from Monte Cassino. The script is unusual. Might Abbot Hrabanus spare you for a short spell?'

If he is surprised nobody would know. He nods, approaches the abbot. Returns and tells her they may walk together to the scriptorium.

'Are you well, brother?' she asks when they are clear of other ears.

'Very well, brother.'

'Only that your complexion speaks of travel in a covered carriage. You must be more important than I knew.'

He does not smile. 'I create more wealth for the abbey with every journey. A covered carriage is the least they can do to thank me.'

'Is it not for God that you collect these works?'

'I thought a man as observant and clever as you would have noticed by now that God does not, in fact, live in Fulda.'

'I was only being light with you,' she says, but it is as if he has not heard.

She risks a longer look, sees dark shadows beneath his eyes, lines carved more deeply than she remembers around his mouth.

'You must be very weary from the journey. Perhaps after you have rested ...'

'It is not the journey that wearies me. It is this.' He flicks his hand at the cloister, the church. At the scriptorium. At her.

'Let us get on with it. Explaining the extremely simple Longobarda script to the cleverest scribe in Fulda will no doubt take considerable time.'

He strides ahead up the stairs and, for the first time in years, she feels an imposter.

She thinks her way out of the dread. There is no rule against friendship, but particular attachments are discouraged. To prefer one brother over the community risks discord. Attachment to earthly relationships prevents true communion with God. That Randulf repels her friendship means she is truly part of the body of Fulda. His refusal to indulge in intimacy is a great compliment and a gift.

She requests permission to work through Terce, Sext, Nones so as to make full use of the low, brief winter light. When the scriptorium is finally too dark, she works in the cloister where there are, at least, wall lamps. When the cloister becomes too cold she retreats to the dorter to work with her blanket wrapped as a shroud, until she is commanded, with the others, to put out her candle and sleep.

Increasingly she finds that in the space between reading a line and replicating it on parchment her mind leaps in to question and argue. Copying Pelagius she realises too late she has allowed her pen to transcribe her thoughts alongside the proper words. A summary of Augustine's original position; a short treatise on why Pelagius misunderstood now interrupts the original text. They are so busy that checking pages before binding is rushed and sometimes not undertaken at all for work by a senior scribe. Still, if someone were to notice her interference, her assumption of scholarship or correction . . . She imagines the denouncement in Chapter. *Step forward, Brother John. Kneel and lift your robe.*

She takes to mouthing each letter to herself as she makes its strokes, as the barely literate scribes of lesser houses are said to do. This prevents her ideas leaking onto the parchment but not from clogging up her mind. Her hand copies with perfection while the rest of her itches to expand on her earlier notes; to explain that Augustine was wrong about predestination though not in the ways Pelagius thought. So hard she strains to keep hand uninfluenced by mind that she forms *S* six times over before noticing. She must scrape the parchment clean before someone sees, thinks her amanuensis to a serpent.

It happens again and again; the accidental commentary on a text she is copying followed by carelessness as she struggles to restrain herself. She loses her place while chanting, glides past the lavabo into the refectory and is called back by Brother Dominicus, who watches her wash as though she were a child caught playing with his own shit. Next Chapter she is ill with fear, but Dominicus remains silent and she—for the tenth, twentieth, hundredth time this winter—promises God she will take more care with His work.

But what if this is the work He wants from her? What if in stifling her thoughts she is denying His call?

She asks Ermo for parchment for her own writing; he sends her to the old parchmenter to beg offcuts. The scraps are thick and uneven, more brown than yellow, edges over-tanned and curled. No matter; their smallness means she can keep one always at the ready beside the texts on her desk. Her thoughts flow smoothly from mind to parchment. At night she orders the scraps, making small piles which trace one argument through to its end, others formulating questions raised, texts to chase down, ideas needing more time. Every thought she releases makes room for a better and more complete one; the messier her pallet becomes with scraps of calfskin, the clearer her mind, the more expansive her thoughts.

God has made me to excel at this work, she thinks. There is not another person on this earth who sees things as I do.

If she were to say this out loud she would be whipped and worse. Insolent and prideful, just as Hatto accused. In herself, she knows it is of God. The intelligence and the awareness of it. There is no greater praise for the Lord than to recognise the wonder of His creation, after all. Her mind—sharper, nimbler, larger than any in this place with more than its share of sharp, nimble, large minds—was made by Him and it would be a sin not to use it as best she can.

No, pride is not her sin. Increasingly, though, anger is. But still on His behalf! That the men who purport to be His most loyal would deny the fullest expression of His creation. That the men who claim to protect His kingdom on earth work to make it smaller and less wondrous. That the true object of their protection is their own sense of power, their prideful conviction in the superiority of their maleness.

For years she has bound and rebound her breasts without emotion. A necessary, uninteresting task like pissing or trimming her nails. Now, as her thoughts break free of the copyists rows, she seethes at the blasphemy of it. Stuffing and strapping and restraining the body given her by the same God who made the mind that the abbey so values.

We are told here, she thinks and thinks and thinks, that bodies are sinful and should be obscured and ignored as much as possible. Yet I, the cleverest and most hard-working of servants, am forced to remember my body in a way I never did when its femaleness was a harmless fact.

In the latrines, while a brother groaningly shits out his lunch on the other side of the wall, she refastens the linen strips around her flattened, rash-splotched breasts and is flooded with a rage so hot and intense she fears it will turn her insides to ash. *God release me from this all-consuming anger,* she prays.

The ways God speaks to us are manifold, Abbot Hrabanus says, and here is a fine example. God calms the raging fire in her but does not, as He surely could, extinguish it. He makes of it a single smouldering coal for her to carry in her heart; a reminder that the only one who matters knows who she is and feels no offence or horror, only hot, live love.

EREMUS

BY THE TIME news of Louis the Pious's death reaches them in Fulda, his sons have plunged Francia into war. Abbot Hrabanus is a friend of eldest brother Lothar and votive masses for his victory are added to the daily office.

God is unmoved by their efforts. Midsummer 841 they get word that Lothar has lost at Fontenoy, though forty thousand men had to die to determine it. It is said the field is so blacked by death the sun stays away so as not to be swallowed whole. The remnants of Lothar's army are pursued by the blood-drunk victors. The woods of Burgundy thicken with the rotting bodies of the men who survived the full force of battle only to have their throats cut as they slept huddled like badgers. If the glorious men of the King's army sometimes slaughter innocent travellers by mistake it is cause for regret, but not overly. Better a hundred dead peddlers than a single living Lotharian.

'That is the end of it,' Abbot Hrabanus announces. He is too famous a supporter of the vanquished for Louis the German—King Louis, it is—to believe in his fealty now. He, their father, retires and she is surprised by the glee some brothers express. She had not known there was dissent or dislike within the abbey. Why would she? She has long since stopped attempting to converse with Randulf and there are no others she trusts well enough to trade gossip. Her only exchanges longer than three or four words are with Hatto and Ermo, and they speak of nothing except their work and hers.

Another surprise, then: Hatto—*her* Hatto—is elected abbot. The surprise is not that he is chosen but that all seem to have expected it. There are murmurs suggesting he has campaigned long for the role, that he wrote in admiration and support of the new king even as the abbey prayed daily for his rival. What else am I blind to in this place? she wonders. What forces gather and swell while I silently mediate arguments between long-dead scholars?

Meanwhile, the Saxons are in revolt, turning the north and east as bloody as the rest of Francia. Meanwhile, God shows the Franks what he thinks of the slaughter wrought by the grandsons of Charles the Great. Weeks of unrelenting rainfall leave the fields of the shattered kingdom sodden and soak the stores which fast turn rotten. And what else follows war and floods but famine and pestilence? And what do famine and pestilence bring but banditry and murder?

The brothers of Fulda, in their well-fortified, heartily stocked, weather-protected home built on the highest ground are spared most of this horror. Occasionally, a man will suggest in Chapter that they might do more to help the wounded, the starving, the terrified, the sick—but the prevailing opinion is that adding more bodies to the ailing masses beyond the walls will be no help at all and, besides, what greater salve for the world's wounds than sincere prayer performed by the purest of souls?

The monks continue to work and eat and sleep and pray. Francia continues to starve and bleed and flood and fester. Soon Fulda's pastures and gardens, too, are sludge. The cellarer reduces rations. The infirmarian stows even the everyday medicines for bone ache and indigestion in his locked chest. Outdoor workers, unable to perform their tasks, take to their knees and pray until their voices are as thin as the pottage served in ever smaller portions.

A month into the unrelenting rain an elder brother complains of a headache at Lauds and is dead by Compline.

'This pestilence is a wolf that has tasted blood,' Ermo mutters after three of his scribes fall sick the next day.

By the end of the week the infirmary is heaving with sickness and the woodward's hands are blistered from digging graves in the waterlogged ground. She watches him from the scriptorium window, tells Ermo it seems a whole pack of wolves has been set loose among them.

By the third week of the sickness, she is alone in the scriptorium, her fellow scribes having died, taken sick or been seconded to more immediately life-sustaining practices: cutting bandages, boiling water, washing sick-soiled linen, preparing pottage and beer more alike in colour and substance than not. Still, Hatto tells them in Chapter, this will pass. The gates will reopen. And when that day comes there must be goods ready for sale.

'Our future health and prosperity are in your hands, Brother John,' Ermo says, before returning to the abbot's cell where his days are spent writing begging letters to the pious rich.

And so, though her hands cramp and ache and her spine feels brittle as new ice, she stays at her desk, does the work of six and then works some more.

'Brother John, may I speak with you?'

Randulf in the doorway, face and voice ragged.

She nods, tells him they are alone and he may speak freely. He approaches her desk, brings the heavy scent of incense with him.

'You are a walking thurible, brother.'

'I have barely left the church this past week. The sub-sacrist has fallen, his assistants, too, and the Requiem Mass ends only to begin again.'

'Father Ermo says—'

'Agnes.'

Her name spoken aloud, like stripping the cowl. Like hot hands against bared skin.

'Agnes.' Again! Like it has never left his mouth. 'I cannot bear the worry one more night. You must leave before it is too late.'

She stretches her arms over her head to stop from covering her face. Braces her hands against each other and cracks out the ache. 'I am taking all precaution,' she says, nodding towards the stack of texts on the empty desk to her right: Dioscorides, Pliny, Hippocrates and Galen. 'I take a decoction of sage, thyme and bitter root daily and keep rue leaves to chew.' She does not tell him about the vervain she keeps in her bed or the vinegar-soaked cloth bound to her chest. Even when he was her friend he would scold her belief in the cures of the market wives. 'I have plentiful stores if you—'

'No, no. This fever, it comes on quickly. By the time you know you are ill you will be too weak to stop them taking you.'

To the infirmary, he means. The illness has been here long enough that a routine is in place, followed strictly. The sick are rolled in blankets and carried to the infirmary courtyard, where they are stripped and both blanket and robes taken to be burnt before the sick man is doused with near boiling water.

Some do not survive the initial treatment. If the infirmarian sees her naked he will make sure she does not.

'I had not thought—'

'While I have thought of nothing else! Truly, only God can know how you do it. Live among us with such ease, as though you have forgotten who you are.'

How to explain that she is more aware of who she is than any man here? That every second of every day and night the binding cuts her flesh and her mind strains to be allowed to do its work? That her entire existence depends on her knowing who she is in order to keep most of herself from sight? If he had not shunned her these last years he might have seen—is the only person who could see—how she has grown, and so seen the way she must conceal an ever larger self.

'The rash comes early,' she says. 'A day or sometimes two before the fever and weakness. If I flee at the first—'

'You will die in the mud or make it to a village only to be uncovered and torn limb from limb by strangers.'

'I will take a horse, make it to Mainz within the day. Find some women's clothes before I seek help.'

'The fever moves faster even than a horse. Especially one of the half-starved creatures in our stables.'

His jaw is set the way it was before she lay with him that day. She is sorry to again be the cause of his torment. She wishes she could tell him this, but since he said her true name the surging mud of the Rhine and the purpling sky have threatened.

'We must pray then, Brother Randulf, that I will have no need to test it,' she says, and his face slackens.

He nods. 'I should like to confirm your continued good health often until this pestilence ends.'

'I should like to do the same,' she says. 'Confirm your health, I mean.'

He nods again and leaves, and the next afternoon he returns and they speak about the copies she has lately been preparing. The next day he returns and reads to her from Virgil while she cuts and pricks parchment. She comments that she will soon run out of ink, and the following afternoon he arrives with a crate of materials which the old monk who whipped her apprentice hands will never use again. He sets up his own ink workshop under the north-facing windows, grinds and stirs and pours while she copies.

She is used to whole days without speaking; she is not used to it taking effort. The air hums with unvoiced words.

By late summer the careful rituals of the abbey are in disarray. With so many sick or dead, bells go un-rung, psalms unsung. It is easy to believe that nobody is watching, on earth or above.

Although the nights are almost as warm as the long, stifling days, and although fire in the scriptorium is forbidden, she builds one in the never-used hearth and feeds it with rosemary and sage in the hope their smoke is stronger than the pestilence. When dark finally falls, she and Randulf sit by its glow and bake like bread as he tells her of his travels these last years, conjures Ravenna and Aachen and Rome and Constantinople, tables overflowing with meat and wine, ladies who wear hats of twisted gold leaf and men who walk bent under the weight of their jewelled belts and sashes.

For hours at a time she forgets to be frightened.

First week of autumn, the air not yet cooled. The prior, a weedy-voiced man with a face as bald and red as a newborn babe, addresses the Chapter meeting. Father Abbot is ill and is being attended in his lodgings by the infirmarian himself. There is no need to say that this situation is preferable to his being taken to the infirmary. The chapter house aches with the spaces left by those dead within days of being admitted to that place.

It is the Feast of the Exaltation of the Holy Cross and there is no abbot to conduct the mass, few brothers to attend. The prior does his best, but the vaulted ceiling devours his every word before it can reach its audience and the red cloak retrieved specially for the service looks from afar as though it is made of his own flushed skin.

Over the coming days the abbey seethes with rumours that Hatto's fever worsens. In the refectory the rule of silence, like almost every rule, has been abandoned and the brothers worry over their bowls of leek water. There is discussion, even, of who might replace their beloved father.

She is making her way across the courtyard, stomach barely less empty than before the meal, when Brother Hermanus sidles alongside her. He is a scribe seconded to the kitchen during the crisis and she has not missed at all his sniffing and throat-clearing, nor his tendency to smirkingly call her Johannes. Now, he addresses her as though they are regular companions, used to talking lightly as they go to their work.

'It seems we may again have to elect a new father,' he says. 'Perhaps this time it will be you, Brother Eugenius.'

The glint in his eye tells her there is no error; he knew her name every time he called her Johannes and he knows it now. Eugenius, he calls her. The woman famously elected abbot of a house she had lived in falsely for many years.

She continues walking, slow and steady. Her chest is bound tight as ever. Head covered, face shadowed. Hands secreted in the sleeves of her robe. There is nothing about her form that could have provoked Hermanus's accusatory misnaming.

'Brother, I worry,' she says, relieved that her voice comes deep and calm. 'You know well that I am John. You have become confused. I fear you may be infected with the pestilence.'

'I am quite well, I assure you.' That sniff, that smirk. 'Only distraught at the misfortune that has fallen on our home and wondering what acts of blasphemy may have brought this blight upon us.'

'The blight is on all the land. It is not ours alone.'

'Indeed. The transgression must be immense for God to punish so many across such great distances.'

'May we continue to live as those deserving of His mercy,' she says, and moves more slowly than she wants to towards the scriptorium and away from his glinting eyes.

Father Eugenius, known now as Eugenia of Rome. Her martyrdom outweighing the sin of her deception. Perhaps God will see fit to arrange such atonement for me, she thinks. Send me somewhere they still cut the heads off Christians. Let me be murdered and my body defiled so I may join others of my sex at His side.

'In case it is not clear, that was a jest, Lord,' she mutters, climbing the stairs. Her voice, deepened even when alone, echoes off the stone. She touches her stomach where the boar ran through. She has read all the texts and said all the prayers and still she does not know which signs to run towards and which to flee.

She is unable to steady her hands enough to work well. She stands and sits, cracks her knuckles, paces the creaking floor. When Randulf comes she tells him of Brother Hermanus's words and the lack of surprise on his face frightens her more than anything else.

'Others know?' she asks.

'Not a soul knows. Including Hermanus.'

'But others suspect. They talk.'

'You are not the only one so discussed. There will always be men who slant girlish. And always men who seek signs of same for their own reasons.'

'What reasons?'

'You must know that not all among our brethren are chaste and some will take a girlish man if no girl is to be found.'

She thinks of the grove. Nothing girlish about those men or that act. What girl would thrust with such violence or hunger with such abandon?

'Do you blush, Brother John?'

She touches her cheeks. 'It may be the fever. You should leave and never come back.'

Oh, but his laugh! Like drinking warmed wine at her father's table. Like lying on the earthen floor with the hearth fire roasting her like a tender young goat.

'Is there a chance,' she says, 'the talk will remain only that?'

'A chance, yes.'

'Not a fair one.'

'In these times, there is a need to place blame.'

'To purge.'

He nods, sad and sorry.

They stand in silence, her face and hands ice-cold again. 'I could take to the road,' she says at last. 'Follow the path of Bachiarius, wander the world for the sake of God,'

'You would become a gyrovague? The most detested of all monks.'

'I have no need of love from brothers nor strangers if I have my freedom.'

'You may not need love but you will need funds. Unless you plan to live the rest of your days crawling around barns stealing slop from unguarded troughs.'

'My belly would be fuller in a night of that than a week of dinners here.'

Lightning flash of a smile. 'War has reshaped the world,' he says. 'Widows are many and scattered far from their marital homes. You could begin again. Go to Aachen or Metz. Rome, even! It is chaos there, easy to melt into the city. You could make a good living as a marketplace scribe. Writing letters, translating documents. As a widow you would be—'

'I am no widow.'

'The lie is small.'

'And I am no market scribbler. I am a Benedictine scholar and scribe and can as well be so in Rome.'

'Rome is not Fulda. It isn't even Mainz, whatever your father told you. You will be found out in an instant, Agnes.'

'That name has become too easy in your mouth. You are more a danger to me than Hermanus.'

She throws a clutch of rosemary onto the fire, breathes deep of the bitter smoke. If she keeps her back to Randulf he will not see that his words have stripped her bare of the past five years, made her again a frightened girl without family or wealth.

'There is Athens,' he says at last.

Athens. She turns the word and the images it conjures over in her mind. City of Socrates, of Plato and Aristotle. The ancient, sin-filled city where St Paul unleashed his love of Christ and disgust with the false idols worshipped by high and low alike, where St Jerome tried and failed to shift the great bronze sphere of Hellenic athletes. It has never occurred to her it is a place that a person could decide to go.

She remembers an etching from a book of her father's—towering columns perched on a rocky hilltop overlooking the sea. There had once been statues of the pagan gods and goddesses standing taller than the walls, but Christian saviours had smashed them with axes and hammers, carved crosses into their marble foreheads and cut out their unseeing eyes.

Justinian closed the schools, drove out the philosophers. That was years ago. Centuries.

In her father's time, the girl who would become empress was born there. Eirene, whose unchangeable, unforgivable sex allowed the Pope and his allies in Rome to split from the east and proclaim Charles the true emperor.

Nothing has happened there since, as far as she knows. It is a place of history. Shabby, provincial. All the serious men of the east, all the brightest, long gone to Constantinople.

'It is a Christian city still?'

'In its way,' Randulf says. 'Which is different enough to ours.'

'But there are monasteries?'

'There are monks. Few live as we do, communally and under the Rule.'

Athens, she thinks. Where being of indeterminate Frankish origin and from a poorly understood religious community would assist her fundamental disguise. All about her would be strange, her smooth-faced maleness the least of it.

'Libraries?'

'More scholars and books than you have known, though they are spread over the city, not . . .' He gestures to the walls around them.

'I could continue my work?'

He sighs. 'You could continue to waste your youth and freedom hunched over manuscripts, yes.'

'I could study Greek,' she says, excitement overtaking fear. 'Properly, Randulf! Come to know it as well as anyone born to it.'

She sees he is amused by her. Swallows back her next words: I can read and think without the interruption of bells and chants. Can discuss ideas with men whose minds have not been shackled by monastic training or bloated by Roman grandiosity.

'It is a long journey,' he says, as though in warning. She hears it as a promise of joy.

'On the sea,' she says; thinks: I will the sail the route of Odysseus and Aeneas, of Scylax!

'Eventually. We will need to leave right away if we're to cross the Alps before winter.'

'We? I am the imposter here, brother. There is no need for you to be exiled too.'

Only a look from him then. His need blazes, a pyre. Five years since he brought her here. Everything has changed for her and nothing at all for him.

APOCALYPSIS

THEY SLIP EASILY through the unmanned gate before dawn, are forced by the miry and untended road to move as slow as winter. The town below is more quiet than it should be even at this early hour. Randulf warned her she would find the world transformed. War and famine and disease have thinned out the towns and made the survivors wary as hares. As though he has not listened to his own warning, he mutters his surprise to find no one about in village after village that first morning. He had planned to buy them a horse in a place half a day's walk from Fulda and is irritated to have to knock on several doors before he can rouse a man willing to conduct business.

Even then the man keeps his distance, holds a cloth wafting camphor over his mouth.

Even then the horse is not one at all, but a donkey, stringy and yellow-eyed.

'Ah, but this is perfect,' Randulf says, beaming. 'What better way to travel than the way of our Lord Jesus, on the back of a humble donkey.'

The man names a price twice that of a strong and healthy palfrey. Randulf's beam brightens. He shines light and flattery and love of God until the man is begging them to take the animal for one-tenth of his asking price and Randulf must insist on paying double that and when they leave, bewildered little donkey ambling between them, the man is shouting great blessings and asking that they return for some bread and ale in better times.

'I had forgotten that you, too, live in disguise,' she says when they are clear of the town.

Randulf looks at her, all sincere confusion.

'Just now I saw the Brother Randulf my father knew. I have not seen nor heard him these five years.'

Randulf laughs loud enough to startle the donkey into stopping. 'Don't we all live as shadow selves in the abbey?' he says, stroking the animal between the ears, urging it forward. 'Are we not all dimmed in there, reduced?'

The donkey gazes up at him with adoration. 'It is in your thrall,' she says.

'Time to see how the poor old thing takes to being mounted, yes?'

Before she can respond he has her by the middle and she is hefted onto the donkey's back. The shock of it: his hands lifting and slinging her like a sack. The animal beneath heaves and squirms and she is in utter sympathy. To be a thing for use, flung or mounted without warning or consent, and he calm and cool as the grass beneath, stroking the donkey's nose once more, telling it that all will be well. Or is it to her he is speaking?

'Shh, my girl, shh. All will be well. You are safe in my hands, and I safe in God's.'

Riding in turn while the other walks they make no better time than if both were on foot, but the little donkey moves smoothly enough to allow the rider to rest for a few hours, at least. Their sleep is rough and brief; there are few inns open and fewer houses willing to answer a stranger's knock, and Randulf is too well known among the monasteries and churches of this country to seek shelter there. If word reaches the abbot (Lord protect him) of their whereabouts he may send a party after them. Or, given the lack of able men, a messenger to spread the word of a bounty for their return.

Like thieves they huddle under trees or in caves, exhaustion winning over fear of bandits or wolves.

They are within a few hours' walk of a river town Randulf knows where they can trade their donkey for passage on a merchant boat. The thought of resting her battered feet while continuing to move south seems worth the animal plus all their remaining coin. Randulf is firm that it is the donkey alone which must pay their passage. There is still so far to travel, and if the snow comes early to the mountains they will need to overwinter in an inn.

The forest trail is narrow here and winds gently downhill towards the sweet hiss of the river. The donkey jerks to a halt, and a breath later the bushes ahead bristle and a clutch of birds takes to the sky in clamouring protest. Randulf dismounts, puts one hand to his knife, the other to hold her back.

Around the bend come two men with bare heads and carrying nothing but a dagger each, held ready in front. They stop three arm-lengths away as more men, in teams of two, emerge behind them. In all, she counts fourteen. Every one looking as though he has run from a midnight fire with barely time to grab his shoes.

'Good day, friends,' Randulf says. 'We are brothers of Fulda Abbey making our way south on monastic business. We go always in peace and would pass by you now unless you would prefer to stay awhile with us as we pray for your safe journey.'

The men in front exchange a look. One lowers his weapon, turns and gestures to the men behind to move to the side of the path. The other keeps his dagger pointed towards Randulf, says, 'You'll need all the prayers for yourselves if it's to the river you're heading.'

'Why would that be, then?'

'Northmen is why,' the man says, and a shudder passes through his group as though the word alone has power to hurt.

It is weeks now, he tells them, since Northmen took Nantes. The duke had been lately killed by a rival and the town laid open for the invaders. They slew the bishop and all his men and, taking those women they liked the look of, made their bloody way down the Loire. It is said they plan to hold Aquitaine for their own. It is unheard of for Northmen not to flee home after their pillage—but, then, never has the world been in such chaos. The foul harvest of the brother war has made a paradise for the piratical.

They step aside to let the band of refugees pass then sit awhile right there on the trail, share a hunk of bread. Let the donkey snuffle at the grass to each side. At last Randulf says, 'We have only lost half a day. We will be back on the road proper by sundown.'

'I hate the road proper,' she says, feeling blood or pus leaking from her heel as she speaks.

'It is a hard way, I know, but one without Northmen and so the one we must take.'

'One look at my feet and the fiercest Northman will crumble in awe and fear.'

'If only.' Randulf heaves himself upright, clicks his teeth to call the donkey in. 'Such savages would likely think your putrid feet a sweet offering. Want to suck at those fetid toes for a bit before chopping you to bits.'

'Your mind is a dark and frightening place, Brother Randulf.'

'Ah, that's nothing. And if you don't get up I'll tell you what else I reckon the Northmen'd enjoy. May even show you if you keep to this lazing about.'

'You're not my abbot,' she says. 'Not my master.'

He shrugs and she stands, winces, begins the slow climb back up to the road.

After eight days of walking the donkey lies down and will not get up. They sit with her until her breath stops and then leave her for the creatures of the forest.

Just past Colmar they exchange greetings with a lone traveller who tells them a treaty has been signed in Verdun, carving up Charles's empire between his grandsons.

'Who then is king where we stand?' Randulf asks.

The traveller shrugs. 'Here's borderlands. Me, I'm for the German. Heading for his territory while I still have a head to guide me. Far be it for me to tell men of God their business, but you'll truly be needing the Lord's protection if you continue on this road. There are those who've not heard the war is finished and those who do not wish it to be.'

They give their blessings to the man and carry on. Within hours, there is another traveller heading north, then a group of six, a trio, another lone man. She wonders if she is destined always to be moving towards that which others are fleeing.

The bread and cheese they packed was not intended to last long. They would fill out the stocks with nuts, herbs and berries from the forest. They had fishing nets and knives for more substantial fare.

Shocking innocence. Even Randulf, who has travelled the world in times of war and peace, has never known the woods to be as barren as the roads. Every tree and bush picked clean by soldiers and refugees. Every creature snared or fled. The streams fouled by year-old corpses, fish rotting alongside. They eat less each day than the one before.

'I would eat that poor donkey in a heartbeat,' Randulf says, and her stomach spasms. They have so quickly become beasts of the forest; no flesh forbidden, no sustenance unholy.

They have been walking more than three weeks. Their supplies long gone and hunger making them slow and thick, they leave the forest road for one that cuts through ravaged paddocks and leads to a village Randulf knows well. It is worth the risks to have a hot meal. To have any meal at all.

Skeletons whole and in parts wait for them there, slayed and devoured in the same place, and who can say if it were wolves or men who'd filled their bellies before the crows came to clean the bones?

The inn Randulf remembers fondly is burnt almost to the ground. They pick through the charred remains, overturning bones and table legs and blackened sticks that could be either. Their desecration is to no end. The place was likely looted before the fire was lit. Not even a blood-drunk soldier with murder in his heart would incinerate something as precious as food.

'I am afraid, Agnes,' Randulf says. 'I think we were killed and now walk through purgatory. Every step is one I've taken before but the ground is ashes and bone and the air stinks of death.'

'Purgatory. That is a comfort. I had thought us already in hell.'

'If it were hell I would be alone here.' He does not look to her for a response. Turns from her, in fact, squats low so his face hovers over part of a rib cage, beside it the corpse of a crow with its beak split like firewood.

'Lord Jesus Christ,' she begins, 'deliver the souls of all the faithful—'

'Agnes. These people may have died unsaved. Still in mortal sin.'

She kneels beside him. The ashes make the ground sickening soft. 'Lord Jesus Christ,' she says again, 'deliver the souls of all the faithful departed from the pains of hell, and the deep abyss,' and after a heaving breath Randulf adds his voice to her prayer.

It is growing dark but this unconsecrated boneyard is no place to rest and so they walk on.

'My father told stories of war but never of what was left behind,' she says.

'Those wars were righteous. Charles the Great winning souls for God.'

'Yes. Merciful savagery. Like King David. Like Saul.' She has heard it again and again. The biblical kings slaughtering whole countries in God's name. Her father—his cause, if not his sword arm—knocking thousands of Jesus-denying heads from necks in Saxony. *Come, behold the works of the Lord; see what desolations He has brought on the earth.*

Would the desecration of all this flesh—every flank and fold of it in the image of Christ—be less terrible if done for the glory of God? Do heathen guts smell sweeter when loosed by a godly sword?

There is a church further along the road, older than the town itself, its walls barely taller than Randulf, built of dark, lumpy rock streaked with iron. Moss grows as it likes on the stones and grass sprouts in the crevices between.

'This at least still stands,' Randulf says, striding towards the dark arch of the doorway.

'Wait. The smell.'

'It only lingers from that last place. Come.' And he is gone into the darkness and she follows, because it is true that to be alone here is to be lost to God and all that is salvable in the world.

Her stomach reacts before her eyes adjust. The pain of an empty gut spasming to void itself folds her over. Her hands find smoothed wood—a bench or altarpiece, she cannot tell. Boiling oil surges up her throat into her parched mouth. When it spills from her lips it is barely enough to wet her chin.

'Agnes. Go.' Randulf has his arms around her, half-lifting her back towards the light.

It is too late. Her eyes have accustomed to the dark and he cannot drag her fast enough to stop her seeing.

Outside they vomit strings of bile onto the dirt. If only a bird would fly overhead. A single cricket chirp. Anything, Lord, to prove that life continues.

Randulf finishes retching first, wipes his mouth and stands. He faces the cursed church, bows his head and begins the prayer for the dead, his voice burnt almost dry. She joins him from her place on the ground, and by the end her stomach has calmed enough she can stand upright.

They backtrack through the town and return to the forest path. A stag—tall as a courser, white as the moon—waits for them around a bend. She stops still; Randulf too. How much can a human heart take? she wonders.

'He could run us both through with a dip of the head,' Randulf says, and the scars on her belly and thigh throb.

Long, breathless moments pass as the stag regards them, a king looking down upon his lowliest subjects. The creature shifts its mighty head as though urging them forward, lopes ahead down the trail.

They follow at a fair distance. The stag's steps are silent; her own collapse piles of half-rotted leaves, create avalanches of sticks and pebbles and tiny bones. In the edge of her vision, Randulf's knife trembles at his side, though his breath comes soft and steady.

Without warning the stag bounds high and leaves the path. At the place he disappeared there grows a sprawling patch of herbs.

We are directly downhill from the church, she thinks. Perhaps some of the blood seeped through the cracks in the stones, soaked into the earth. She chews the tender leaves slowly, swallows with care. She will not let her stomach reject this. Mint and sorrel, sweeter than any she has tasted. Gifts from the dead.

On the road approaching Valence, there is the miracle of an open ale house. The owner does not ordinarily take lodgers, but he is devout and so allows passing brothers use of a narrow partitioned space behind the kitchen.

There is a meal of stewed beans and weak ale, and then Randulf complains of a headache, says he will go straight to his rest.

She nods him on his way and orders another cup of ale.

'We have an early start, Brother John,' he says. 'I trust you will not carouse until all hours.'

'Never fear, Brother Randulf. I shall be as fresh as a milkmaid come morning.'

She drinks slowly but for many hours, and by the time she makes her way through the empty kitchen her head dips and spins and she cannot help making a racket as she stumbles behind the curtain and lands hard on the pallet where Randulf lies.

'You took your blessed time,' he says, and the moon shows his bitter face and his bared chest.

How long since she has seen living flesh? Even her own has become a mystery. Bound and robed and draped in the dark.

'Do you expect me to share a pallet with you in this state?' she asks.

'Would you have me sleep in my filthy clothes this first night in thirty in which I have warmth enough not to?'

'As you like.'

She removes her shoes, takes his cloak from the floor and lies down in its place, letting the damp and stinking thing fall over her.

'Agnes. Please.'

Two words and they could have been any at all and still she'd know he was saying, *Save me.*

She lies still, though the ale in her makes the ground tilt. She listens to Randulf's breath, her own. Is it a miracle they breathe or an abomination that she should wonder at it?

'*The days are coming,*' Randulf murmurs, '*when people will say, Blessed are the barren women, the wombs that never bore, and breasts that never nursed. They will say to the mountains, Fall on us! and to the hills, Cover us! For if they do these things in the green wood, what will be done in the dry?*'

She closes her eyes and sees charred bones. Yellow bones. Bleached bones, her own from a long-ago dream.

'*I will praise you Lord with all my Heart—*' she begins.

'God is gone from us, Agnes.'

The grief in his voice opens a pit which could swallow her whole. God help me, she prays. Help us and hold us safe.

'He is here as surely as we are.' As she says it she knows it to be true.

'After what we saw today? No.'

How to explain that she understands nothing of what she has seen but her body hums with certainty that it was God who showed it to her, who led His fleeing servants through the valley of death, brought them to this moonlit cell where she can feel Him in every miraculously ordinary breath, in her still-beating heart, her warm rushing blood? If there is Scripture or prayer, liturgy or commentary that has put words to the truth her body holds then she has not yet read it.

So she stands and, with her back to Randulf, removes her robe and shift. The air is cool against her too-hot skin. Randulf's breath a wild stampede.

When she turns his breath catches. 'Oh. Oh, Agnes. What has happened?'

'A boar,' she says. 'I was a child. God was there with me. He let it happen. I didn't understand why at the time. But I knew He was there, as surely as I know it now.'

Randulf moves to his knees. 'Does it pain you?'

'Not for many years.'

He skims his palm over the thick cords of her scars. For weeks he has handled her like a satchel he is obliged to transport. Hauling her on and off the donkey without warning, heaving her across creeks and up steep embankments. Out of that cursed church. Only now does she think, Oh! I had forgotten what it is to be touched.

'Not even Adonis survived the boar,' he says as his palm circles and circles.

'Adonis did not have God.'

'No.'

'And we do.'

'Yes.' More a breath than a word.

His hand has stoked a heat she can neither stand nor do without. She thinks to tell him to stop, yet what comes from her is a raw-throated cry which he answers in kind. She pushes him to the pallet as he tears at her bindings and they wrangle there until she is beneath him and he enters her as he did long ago in Mainz, but this time they are skin to skin and he says her name and holds her gaze and she could die from this feeling.

'No. Like dogs,' she says, and his eyes near roll back in his skull as he pulls out and turns her. He finishes almost as soon as he starts, bucking like a parody of a beast.

He rolls her over again, presses his mouth to her scar. Kisses her there until she forgets every gristled bone, every wet and rotting fragment she's seen this terrible day. Becomes a creature of hunger and instinct that knows to shift its hips until his tongue finds its proper place and laps at what must be her coursing blood and she is running and running and knows the stream is close and then she lifts clean off the earth and is a comet soaring, burning hotter with each second until she combusts, is nothing but scattered heat and light.

At dawn he watches her strap her breasts, runs his fingers light as spider web over her scars.

'At last I understand why your father could not marry you. It has been a true mystery to me all these years.' He strokes the callused skin like it is fourfold woven silk. 'God marked you for greatness.'

She brushes his hands away, secures her binding.

'Without this you would have been rushed into wifedom before you were full-grown. He spared you from death and from a life of womanly sorrow and servitude so that your mind would not be wasted.'

'Indeed? Did He tell you that Himself, Brother Randulf?'

A smile from the before-times, from sun-bright walks through Mainz. The smile of a precocious young monk for an innocent girl, neither having prayed over a nation's worth of corpses in one terrible day.

'He made sure I found you the way He makes sure I find the finest manuscripts. He knew I would see your true value.'

'May the Lord cut off all flattering lips,' she says, finishes dressing, tells him to get moving. There is still much walking ahead and she is ravenous as a king.

They have passed through purgatory, it seems, and now, at the part of the journey which is supposed to be most difficult, they find they move through paradise. Every day in the Alps there is sun to cheer their spirits and sweet mountain air to keep them cool. Every day there is a stream bursting with fish, a forest thick with herbs, fruit and nuts, a trader's cart with salty meat and tangy cheese, soft white bread and cold ale. Every day there is a moment she judges them clear enough of others to push Randulf to the ground and ride him like the horse she is determined to procure as soon as they reach Athens.

'I cannot decide if you are devil or angel,' he says after one such coupling, his curls strewn with pine needles, his face mottled and sweat-soaked. 'Such torment and transcendence wrought by the same being.'

'I might say the same of you.'

His face contorts with joy and at once her body clenches in desire, though moments ago she sated it so fully.

'Back in Mainz you told me—do you remember?—you told me that it is better not to know this pleasure at all, that to know it is to want it forever more.'

'And yet you didn't. You said, in fact, you would never lay with me again. Not if I talked at you for a thousand days.'

I was newly an orphan, she thinks, my poor father not dead a week. And only a girl, besides, when you trampled me in the mud beneath your desire. I did not know—how could I?—that the desire could be mine, that its satisfaction need not cause grief but be a salve for it.

'Oh, I meant it most sincerely,' she tells him. 'I can only conclude you have worked some foul charm on me while I slept. Truly, since Burgundy I am more goat than girl.'

He makes the mistake of revealing the full raw length of his throat to her as he laughs, thereby ending any possibility of further travel that day.

In Marseille, at last, they take a room on the top floor of a sailor's inn. The door locks and the men drinking and brawling below are louder than thunder. They have weeks—perhaps all of winter—to wait for a ship sailing east, and the innkeeper thinks them the most pious of men the way they eat early and retire to their room to pray and keep themselves safe from the temptations of the night-dark city.

And they do pray, kneeling side by side. Why would they not, when God has not only delivered them safely to this port but also to each other? They pray sincerely and joyfully and then, with equal sincerity and joy, find new ways to worship the magnificence of God's creation as manifested in these two sun-scoured and road-roughened and blessedly, miraculously alive bodies.

Still, the unguarded moments before sleep hold horrors. Blackened bones. A child's face near obliterated by maggots. The smell of rotting innards in her nose, boiling oil in her throat. She reaches for Randulf and he is there, always, to help her to oblivion.

Sometimes she is enraged by how simple it is. Simple and sublime and denied to her all these years.

If she had known back in Mainz that there was no end to the ways in which two people might couple, that she need not be grass trodden beneath pounding feet, that she might move to better please herself and that this would in turn please the other, and that his heightened pleasure would heighten hers and that this could go on and on, spiralling ever upwards in the combined and exultant effort of it. If she had known that then, ah.

Then she would have married, yes. Randulf, if he could escape the abbey; another man if not. Soon there would be a babe in her belly and no books other than household accounts, if her husband let her attend to them at all.

So. Half a decade without this pleasure but for the best after all. Randulf, her truest friend and champion. The reason she is now more educated than he, more skilled in Latin and Greek, more likely to find work as a scribe and perhaps even a place in a school in Athens. Randulf, who has always loved her mind and, now that she has invited him to love her body, does so with enthusiasm and ever-increasing skill, always taking care not to spill his seed where it might start a child.

Randulf, who—perhaps it is a shame or perhaps another gift—likes to speak in between acts of love. And so, though they share long hours in which she is more free than the birds, his talk of Athenian men and eastern monks and the ways in which she must behave on ship in order to continue her glorious fraud reminds her that this scarred and secret body is still earthbound, that this man can take her to a place of momentary rapture but can never take her out of the womanly form with which she is burdened.

TEMPEST

WINTER ENDS AND overnight the dock and surrounding streets are crammed with dealmakers and slavers, the captive and the fleeing. It is a morning's work only to secure places on a trading ship eager for both the coin they offer and the protection that must surely come from having God's men aboard. Protection is sorely needed in these times, the captain tells them. The seas through which they will travel are teeming with raiders and pirates, and many previously safe ports have lately fallen to enemies of Christendom.

They leave at dawn, which here in the south breaks harsh and all at once. Standing on deck in full night dark, she blinks against the salt sting, opens her eyes to the white light of day.

Shouts go out and the boards beneath her feet, the ropes overhead, the very substance of the earth surge.

'*This sea! Great and broad of hands!*' she shouts, and Randulf squeezes her arm, begins to sing the Psalm from the beginning: '*Bless the Lord, O my soul, O Lord my God, You are very great clothed with splendour and majesty,*' and she joins him in song as the shipmen sweat and shout until the dock is a shimmering line and then nothing at all.

Nine days into the journey, through which they have been blessed with fine weather and good winds, a storm rushes at them from the clear blue sky. Randulf, laughing, says, 'Pray they don't cast lots to find which of us God is punishing.'

She laughs with him, though her insides surge as high and fast as the sea. I am a child of the river, she tells herself. There is nothing to fear in the water.

A wave engulfs their little vessel, recedes long enough for her to empty her stomach, engulfs, recedes, and the call of man overboard becomes a scream as a new wall of water collapses. A river is not an ocean, and dear God, I understand that there is everything to fear for those who forget to fear You. Forgive me, she prays, and Randulf catches her arm, holds tight, as the boat is lifted towards heaven, then dropped near on its side so the water need not even leap to cover the deck.

RAPTURE

—

She wakes to bird calls and a breeze stinging her face. Her cloak is heavy with sea water and her mouth tastes of vomit and salt. The improbably blue sky burns her eyes.

'Praise the Lord! He wakes!' Randulf's voice loud and joyous, then his mouth close to her ear, his whisper, 'My Agnes. I thought you lost to me. My beloved. My world.'

There is a man behind and another on her left. Randulf on her right. They lift her until she is seated and her head may as well be at the bottom of the sea. Her stomach heaves, but there is nothing to expel.

'Truly, brothers, your presence has been a great blessing,' the captain says. 'A tempest to beat them all and only three men lost. God's work indeed. God's work.'

The stock is all gone, of course, the boat held together with sea foam and prayer. They will put up at the nearest port and send word to Marseille. With luck, the owner will forward funds for repairs. Still, the brothers may wish to make other arrangements. The wait could be long and end in orders to return home rather than continue east for one-sided trade.

The port, as it happens, is on the island of Malta, the very same where St Paul landed when the ship taking him as prisoner to

Rome was blown off course and wrecked. It is a sign, no doubt, but of what, she does not know.

The local priest accepts them into his church, which is little more than a barn with a crate for an altar and, above it, a cross formed by two pieces of rough wood equal in length. He shouts across the road in a language neither understands, and soon a young nun in a pale blue habit brings them bowls of salty fish stew. When the meal is done, the priest indicates a pallet in a cupboard near the door. In awkward Latin he tells them the church must stay locked. Dogs and bandits are a problem, it seems. He kisses the key around his neck, hands it to her reverently. He will retrieve it in the morning when, they understand, they will be expected to leave.

The priest's shuffling steps have not fully faded into the night when Randulf lifts her as a child and carries her to the pallet. 'My beloved, my world,' he says, kissing her face and throat. 'Oh, I thought you lost to me.'

If she closes her eyes she is back on the boat, her body rocked violently by a terrible, inhuman force. She opens them and it is worse. The force that moves her comes from within this man. Within her, as well. It is more wrecking than any storm, this pulse this press this clutch this need.

'Agnes Agnes Agnes,' Randulf says, and perhaps she says his name or perhaps it is God's. *Unto Him with my mouth I have called, And exaltation is under my tongue.* It is difficult to know what is prayer and what blasphemy, what terror and what joy.

Three men died and she did not, and now, in the place where St Paul sheltered with his captors, she is fast approaching rapture, and whether it is the same experienced by the lowest beasts or by Solomon in his garden is unknown, is unimportant.

'Ah! My Agnes! Ah!' Randulf is still, his face a death mask. Too late she feels the hot pulse where their bodies link. His promise to never spill his seed where it could flourish is more sacred to her than any witnessed vow. Yet here she lies, the liquid snare inside her.

'I thought you dead,' he says. 'My love, my wife, my life. Long hours I thought it and wanted only that another storm would come and take me too. It was a greater grief than I have ever known.'

He collapses his full weight onto her and his lamentations soon ease into snores. She is pinned fast and it feels his thumping heart comes from within her own punished chest. She strokes his head and thrums with his heartbeat and breathes his breath. She shifts her hips as much as his weight allows, hopes the seed that leaks cold onto her thighs hasn't already done what the tempest could not.

The fault is not Randulf's. He has never pretended to be other than a man forced to live as a monk. Why should he, that unwilling child oblate, hold her discipleship more highly than he holds his own? Why should he care to preserve her body for the monastic life when he has spent a lifetime wishing to free his from the same?

The error is all hers. She prayed that God would spare her from marriage and childbearing, and lately she thanks Him for this gift by mouthing pretty prayers that pretend her relentless rutting is a form of worship and not a refusal to contemplate the darkness of this fallen world.

Oh, she yearns towards God from beneath her sleeping lover. *Oh, to have an undivided self, an undivided heart!*

After some time Randulf rolls away and at once she rises and slips on her cloak. Its sea stink makes her gag but there is no time to rinse it clean or find another. She carries her sandals in one hand, her satchel in the other. The church door is blessedly quiet, the moon blessedly bright. Lord, protect Randulf and help him see the rightness of this, she prays, already running in the direction of the docks.

It is an easy enough thing to find a vessel to take her away from this port and to another. Any other will do. It is the away that matters, for now. As she waits on the deck of an island-hopping ship a third the size of the one she boarded in Marseille, the parts of her still bruised from the storm recruit her heart to their protest. To sail again is a horror they will not stand.

RAPTURE

She waits on deck as the crew loads the last of the goods around her and her heart bucks against leaving, but her mind, still struggling free of the poppy-laced wine of Randulf's love, knows there are far worse horrors than drowning all at once at sea.

THERE SHE BECAME
PROFICIENT IN A DIVERSITY
OF BRANCHES OF KNOWLEDGE,
UNTIL SHE HAD NO EQUAL

(842-849)

WOLF MOUNTAIN

SHE IS A skeleton bound in salted hide. Her chest sunken as any man's who has spent months vomiting up all of his food and most of his water. Her feet enflamed with burst pressure sores, legs spindled as a newborn kid. At each port Christians appear to carry the suffering monk in their carts or sling him gently over mules, beg him to stay in their camp, their home, their guesthouse overnight, to be allowed to wash his putrid feet and spoon broth between his crusted lips before the next terrifying, sick-making stage of the sea journey.

She is not aware she has reached Athens until she hears the man who has placed her corpse-weight onto yet another cart tell the driver his passenger is to be delivered to the monastery at the base of Wolf Mountain. Words Randulf breathed into his sex-drugged lover's ear in Marseille, repeated by her like a prayer through months of delirium, transubstantiated now into clear direction from Venetian sailor to Hellenic porter.

The cart careens over stones the size of her head, each jolt stunning her bones anew. I will write to him, she thinks. I will give him that much, at least: the knowledge that I live still.

But if he knows he may come. Come and reclaim her and this time, perhaps, she will give in to his want for a wife, her own depraved want of earthly love. Perhaps this time his seed will take root, flourish and all will be lost.

She stares up into the blistering sun until the light obliterates all.

Her vision and wits return slowly. She is seated on a bench of stone. Someone drips water on her lips, holds a cold cloth to her brow. Strong, musky incense fails to disguise the smell of rotting flesh but is welcome anyway. She focuses on the scent, lets it draw her further into this room which is cool and dim, the walls and floors washed with white. Men in blue robes and long beards move so quickly around her she can't tell if there are three of them or more. They murmur in Greek and click their tongues and pass a vessel, a pot, a box back and forth.

A man the others call Abba kneels in front of her, washes her feet. His beard is the colour of the walls, his face like just-cracked ice, though his hands move with the ease and strength of youth. 'I will ask our herbalist for a potion for the suppuration,' he says in Latin. 'But first these novices will take you to the bathhouse and scrub your travels from your flesh.'

Sharpened in an instant, she sits straighter. Randulf warned her of eastern bathhouses. Not wilfully wanton places like in Rome, but a danger all the same. It is a rare man who can truly keep his eyes down when surrounded by the naked flesh of his brothers.

'Abba,' she says, 'I thank you, but my order demands modesty.'

'Of course.' He smiles, a father humouring his foolish child. 'I will have a sitting bath prepared and ensure you are undisturbed.'

The bathhouse is carved into the base of the mountain. Limestone walls and floor and four wooden tubs, each large enough for several men. The servant who brought her here told her she should make use of them all, which strikes her as decadent until she sees the sweet-smelling water blacken as she sinks into it. She stays awhile in the cooling filth, gathering strength before climbing into the next tub. Only in the final bath does the water stay clear and reveal her body in all its starved and pristine wrongness.

The servant has left her a shift and robe, both of blue linen so soft she might be wearing a cloud. She is escorted to another mountain-carved cell, where a table is laid with olives and figs, dark, gamy meat, white cheese and warm bread. 'All things are clean to the clean,' Abba says, urging her to take from every plate.

As she eats—slow and careful, her stomach shrunk to that of a gnat—men dressed in robes like hers (though some soiled enough to appear Benedictine at first sight) join the feast. Most of them speak a Latin so mangled as to be almost another tongue, though a very few have the accent and grammar of Roman scholars. She urges them to speak Greek, and then she is the one with shameful grammar and clumsy pronunciation, but nobody minds. The men want to know every step of her journey, every detail of her life in the distant and strange western empire. It is just as St Paul found eight centuries ago; the men of Athens like nothing more than to hear something new.

She speaks more in these hours than she has in months, and when exhaustion hits she is led across grounds scented by things she has no names for and into another limestone cell with a mattress almost as thick as the one she had as a child.

'We are not a monastery as you understand it,' Abba tells her in the morning over more warm bread and olives under a tree outside the hut where she was greeted yesterday. 'We are a community of monks who value contemplation and service to God above all else. The manner of such contemplation and service will be different for each. After all, God does not ask the fish to fly nor the bird to swim.'

She is welcome to stay in the guest cell, Abba tells her, or to wander their valley and beyond to find a place that sings to her soul. For instance, he says, there is a modest hut on the edge of the valley. Its previous occupant has lately abandoned the community to return to his family, leaving the hut open to any man willing to care for a small clutch of chickens and a family of goats.

So it is that her mornings are spent milking goats and gathering fresh eggs. At first her enfeebled body must rest for hours after each task, but soon she is strong enough to finish it all before the sun is fully overhead and then spend the afternoons perched at a high table by the front windows copying lives of the saints for local scholars who pay handsomely for texts produced in fine Carolingian minuscule.

When the light begins its soft and gradual fall, she puts aside her work and walks across the valley to deliver the day's bounty to the communal cellar, then continues up the hill until all of Athens is sprawled beneath, the dark gleaming Aegean at its edge. Feels again as she did in the Fulda library, in the room in Marseille, for the first moment on deck of the ship: that God has blessed her truly by placing so much of His glorious creation in her path.

At nightfall she drags her work table outside beside an ancient, fragrant stone pine and loads it with her portion of the blessings of the day: fresh vegetables from the garden, eggs and milk, as well as whatever her new friends bring from their own allocations. In bursts of two or three they come down the hill and across the valley, arguing among themselves or laughing and singing or sometimes all of these at once. One may carry a freshly roasted rabbit, another a fish stew. Sometimes there is bitter wine the colour of stream water, sometimes a sweet rich ruby drink far less strong but so much more palatable that all around the table are equally drunk by the end of the night.

Sometimes she forgets that the table is hers, that she sits at its head, that it is her attention the men compete to attract with their outrageous blasphemies or pious righteousness. Sometimes—warm air on her skin, soft light making spritely shadows, belly and head full to bursting—she suspects she has fallen asleep at her father's feet. If she stands or speaks the dream will dissolve; she will be scolded and sent to her bed.

When her visitors leave each night and she attempts to sleep she is besieged by thoughts of Randulf, who should be here, living as he yearned to do, as both her husband and her brother. She should write to him. She cannot.

RAPTURE

At least, having a hut of her own, she can keep the candle burning all night. She can strip off her shift and bindings and rub oil into the heat rash and welts. She can talk to God without the formalities of public prayer, ask Him to explain the Pantheon, built by pagans for a pagan goddess, now the church of Theotokos, the Mother of God. She has taken to walking there before the morning's work, and as the sun rises it flits and twirls between the columns, and though she knows it is an illusion, every time she feels sure that the building itself is dancing.

To build temples open to the air as these ancients did seems right, she tells God. To view the sun, the stars while praying, rather than stone. What were you thinking, Lord, she asks, leaning her blissfully bare chest out of the window, in allowing pagan men worshipping false gods to create spaces of pure divinity? I know it is not Satan who gave these men such inspiration. The creation is too pure, too holy. I know these places as Yours. But how did they become so at the minds and hands of men who sacrificed goats and prayed to slabs of marble? Why use the hands of sinners to create monuments to heaven?

Ah, and why allow me, Lord, sin-soaked and false, to enjoy such glory and grace every day?

By winter—which hardly deserves the name here, the days barely cooler and shorter, the nights occasionally cold enough to require a single fine-woven blanket—men of religion and academia are crossing the city to visit the hut of the man known as the Benedictine, the Frank, Brother Ioannes, John the English.

Priests and scholars and scribes from the city monasteries come to interrogate her on the *filioque* controversy, which has been stewing tepidly for at least five centuries and which, as a good western Christian, she declares not a controversy at all. The Holy Spirit proceeds from the Father and the Son together, she tells and retells the gathered men. That they continue to ask for her opinion means they must doubt their own, she teases. Either that or they enjoy poking their little Frankish bear to make him dance.

March 843. She has been in Athens a little more than a year when news reaches their community that Empress Theodora has restored the icons of Constantinople. The younger men around her table are all delight, full of plans to bring *this* fresco painter from Rome, *this* famed illuminator from Naples. The older ones weep and wring their hands as they tell of seeing the Christ child washed over with lime and St Paul smashed to dust. Can you imagine, they implore the younger men, the torment of watching some imperial brute scrape away Mother Mary's beloved face with a filthy hunk of pumice? Better to wait and see if this edict lasts rather than commission the artists. Better to worship within blank walls than to experience again such mutilation and destruction.

Ten years ago, she thinks and cannot say, a young monk asked for my thoughts about iconoclasm and it was the most extraordinary thing. I could not have conceived this greater marvel, still, that one day I might sit with the men whose case I so earnestly argued at my father's table. Lord, you have made a wonder of my little life. What astonishments beyond this moment's imagining do you have in store for me yet?

Word of Brother John's charisma and hospitality grows. By her third year in Athens it's not unusual for there to be a dozen men at her table and the same again sprawled on the ground beneath the stone pine. Teachers from the largest junior school in Athens come often to argue with those from the senior school about whose role is more important in shaping the minds and characters of the future leaders of the empire, only to unite, after a certain amount of wine, in railing against those who choose private tutors for their sons. Always, there are at least two or three such tutors at table, and if one of them is George Constantine or all of them are drunk the schoolmasters will finish the night with bloody noses.

As long as he is not provoked by public schoolteachers, George Constantine is a mild, good-humoured man who made his fortune teaching the sons of royalty in Alexandria and Antioch. He speaks of Athens like Hrabanus spoke of heaven; makes it easy to believe he chooses to be in this outpost, teaching the children of merchants by day and drinking with monks and schoolteachers by night. Perhaps. Or perhaps, as the gossip said, he was driven from Antioch in disgrace for laying with his students or their mothers, or both.

The monks say gossip is devil talk and then methodically milk every drop of intrigue and scandal from the city men at table. Hours are spent on the infant emperor Michael and whether it is his mother or the eunuch Theoktistos who wields the power in the imperial palace. More hours still on whose wife turned up to the agora in silks beyond her husband's means and whose garden this prominent teacher or that pious priest has been secretly tending.

Most of all, the monks of the community gossip about whichever of them is not present: Brother Romanus takes double portions of bread and cheese from the cellar; Brother Nikolas spends so long bathing his skin is permanently shrivelled; on certain nights Brother Damianus leaves his cell stark naked and shouts obscenities at the moon but Abba will not intervene as Damianus's father donates near half of the community's funds, without which Abba would not be able to keep three servants as well as a handful of spritely young novices.

What do they say of Brother John when I am absent? she wonders. In her hearing they say he is so clever you would not know he was a Benedictine, so refined in manners you would not believe him a Frank. George Constantine says he knows a dozen families who would pay handsomely to have the English monk tutor their sons. Brother Theodore says the novices speak of almost nothing else than these forbidden-to-them gatherings. At least half of the boys who come to join the community, Theodore says, are driven by the desire to join Brother Ioannes's table rather than to serve God.

She does not know what they say when she is not present and increasingly she does not care. Each day she copies and translates texts from every corner of the empire, and with no one watching over her shoulder is able to read as slowly as she likes, to make notes and sometimes copies for herself. She walks through the Acropolis at dawn and her thoughts expand to fill the space around her. She climbs to the top of Wolf Mountain at dusk and ideas swoop like eagles. At her table each night she launches them back into the air, testing their hardiness and loftiness both. To a man, her companions take every utterance with equanimity, arguing robustly but never censuring. Her ideas fly and fly. They soar.

Her fourth year in Athens, a typically warm night, a full moon the colour of bone overhead.

A scholar recently returned from Ravenna brings news that Saracen forces have sacked Rome this summer just passed.

'Whatever for?' says George Constantine. 'Surely there is nothing left worth taking in that tired town.'

There is laughter at this, though it is evident that some laugh in agreement while others take it as a joke that a man in Athens—of all sad, depleted outposts!—would disparage Rome in this way.

Some are not laughing at all. A grammarian whose name she forgets, despite him reintroducing himself each time he comes, is outraged. 'Do you even know what it is you mock?' He slams his little fists on the table, spilling wine and making George Constantine laugh harder. 'The resting place of our St Peter—yes, you scandalous atheists: our St Peter—this sacred site pillaged by Saracens. Saracens! The church of St Paul desecrated as well. The crosses torn off the walls and used for the devil only knows what purpose. It is a monstrous attack on every Christian. You should all be ashamed. Ashamed!'

His fists pound again. The wine jug, having been emptied during his rant, rolls about harmlessly.

'Brother John, do you have nothing to say on this?' The grammarian is wet-eyed, raw-voiced. 'Your Benedictine brother sits on the throne of St Peter. This pretender enjoying his worldly riches while the eternal riches of our church are pillaged and destroyed!'

'I have no great love for Sergius,' she says. 'Nevertheless, it is vile to laugh at the desecration of any holy site. Barbaric, in fact, to speak lightly of such an attack. As though a city is a block of stone rather than a community of living beings.'

'You are quite right, brother,' one of the loudest laughers says, sombre and contrite. 'We must pray for the souls of those killed by the invaders.'

'The Frank calling us barbarians!' Constantine scoffs, but he is alone in his merriment now. The others have bowed heads, praying—or pretending to, at least.

She too has bowed her head. She thinks: These men turn to me as an authority. Prays: Lord, protect the holy city of Rome and your faithful children living within her walls. Thinks: I should like to see Rome before it is gone forever. Thinks: Look how they all wait to speak, drink, smile, laugh, eat. Look how they all look to me.

ANASTASIA THE PATRICIAN

MIDSUMMER, HER FIFTH year in Athens. Unusually, she is attending Abba's table tonight. It is a feast day—they have twice as many in the east—and locals hoping to widen the narrow path to heaven have inundated the community with cheeses and fruit, wine and fish. It seems every monk in the valley is around the table, crammed tight so their shoulders bounce against each other and their hands touch as they reach for food and goblets. She is grateful to have been seated at the right hand of Abba, since the most hermitic and therefore unwashed brothers are made to sit at the far end of the very long table.

Even so, the sour gaminess of men's bodies packed together on an airless night reminds her powerfully of her first nights at Fulda. It seems an age since she was there, since she has thought of it even. At once she is with Randulf in the scriptorium as he begs her to flee, stepping over bones in Burgundy, laughing with the immensity of their shared pleasure in Marseille. A heartbeat later she is abandoning him on a church floor. The pain of it is smaller than she thought it could ever be and that is a sorrow in itself. Lord forgive me and keep him safe, she prays in the midst of the feast, wishing she'd paid attention to which saint they were feting, so she could ask for intercession.

She opens her eyes and across from her is the angel who holds Christ's clothes in the painting to the left of the St John the Baptist altar in the crypt of the Ugesberg chapel in Fulda: black ice eyes round as the moon, skin like thrice-smoothed lindenwood, red-ochre lips and, suffusing it all, a pure and golden light. Are you here to intercede for my poor Randulf? she almost says, but then the angel stands and reaches across the table, grabs a wedge of bread and shoves it whole into his great red maw. He is as much cherub as she is unicorn.

'Ah, Brother John, you have not met Antony who has joined our community this very week,' says Abba, and she realises she has been staring. 'He has the manners of a goatherd but his love of God is powerful, his hunger for communion immense.'

Powerful. Immense. Abba might have been describing Antony's hands, each large enough to crush her skull with ease.

'Brother Antony,' Abba calls, 'you must meet our esteemed brother, John of England.'

Antony pauses mid-chew. Crumbs rest a moment on his chin before his tongue—thick and wide as a bull's—sweeps them back into his gob. He swallows and the swell of his throat sends a hot surge of blood through her own.

'I am deeply honoured to be in your company.' His Greek is childish, clumsy, but his voice resonates in her chest and as he bows his head in her direction she smells sweet fermenting apples.

'It is always a pleasure to meet another who has travelled great distances to be in this wondrous place,' she says, and his smile casts all else into shadow.

'Not as far as you, Father. England is so distant I can only dream it.'

'I am no father, brother, and I too have never seen England. Tell me—'

An urgent pull on her arm from the old monk on her right. He is engaged in a heated discussion about the Paulicians and begs her aid. This man, whose name she has long forgotten, always assumes the barbarian monk will support his bellicosity, always acts newly shocked that she condemns swords and fire as a first resort. He is an old man but has clearly never seen war or its ugly aftermath. That a Christian with differing views is better off headless is an easy opinion if you have never had to see the insides of a severed neck.

So, she speaks to these innocent, unworldly monks in the way her father once spoke to the men at his table, the way Hrabanus spoke to the more arrogant among his flock: she questions this assumption then that, urges this man to return to his Bible and that one to read his history. Urges all involved to spend more time in prayer. Not one of those men listening raptly seems to notice the tightness in her frame, the way she braces herself against the new tilt of the earth. If she relaxes for even a moment she will slide directly into Brother Antony's lap.

Brother Antony comes to her hut, asks if she might tutor him in Greek.

'Almost every other man here speaks Greek from birth. You are better learning from one of them.'

'Grammar then. Or Psalmody. Mathematics or . . . I have everything to learn. Everything, Fa—Brother Ioannes.'

'Please, I am John,' she says in Latin. 'And we may speak our common tongue when we are alone. Now sit awhile.' She gestures to the bench beside her. 'Tell me, brother, why it is you are here?'

He looks at her with such intensity she is sliced with fear. 'Last night as I tried to sleep, God struck me.' He thumps his chest. 'And though my eyes were closed I saw your face.'

'I meant,' she says, amazed at the calm of her voice, 'what brought you to Wolf Mountain?'

He tells her then of his childhood in Campania, where war and hunger were the only constants. He saw his mother die of fever when he was four and his father to Lombard raiders when he was twelve. He escaped with his sister, who died days later from lack of food or perhaps disease or loss of hope. It all looked the same to him. Alone, he found his way to a monastery that took him in as a horse hand.

'My body took warmth from the horses, my soul from the chanting of the monks. I worked ten years to be allowed to enter the monastery proper. I had just begun my noviciate when the Saracens raided. Again, I survived through God's grace, escaped to Crete, made my way to Thessalonica doing what I could to earn bread and passage. What I must.' His voice is heavy with grief and shame and she wants to kiss his forehead and offer forgiveness for whatever sins he committed to survive.

'It was there I heard of this place where all men are welcome so long as they have a heart for God. I came at once and I will never leave. This is my home until the Lord takes me.' His eyes are locked on hers as though she is this place he speaks of. As though they together here under this tree are the home he has found. He says, 'Tell me what your journey has been, Brother John.'

She tells him all, leaving out only the fact of her disguise and carnality of her friendship with Randulf. She tells of the pagan mother killed by birthing her, the English priest who raised her and the earthquake that took him. The friend who found her a place at his abbey despite her lacking the funds or lineage. The fever that spread through that place and the decision to leave. The hunger and horror of the journey. The storm which spared her life at sea. The way she continued on, despite not knowing or much caring, some days, which side of death she lay upon.

'Ah,' Brother Antony says. 'This is why God has drawn us together so powerfully. You too know what it is to wonder why you are still here while all those you love are gone to Christ.'

'Yes.' She places her hand where the boar failed to end her. 'Perhaps we are supposed to help each other, Brother Antony, to find the answer.'

A typically sultry night and the younger men are sprawled on the grass while she and some older monks talk around the table. A glance to the side and there is Antony, his attention not on his fellows but resting hotly on her ankles. Her mind floods with images of what might happen were she to keep him here tonight, reveal her true form. His fevered excitement, the boundless, animal hunger. Him speaking shock while he rides her to a lather.

And then he would kill her for it.

Or he wouldn't and that might be worse. She cannot bear to start over again, alone and afraid.

She resettles her robe to fully conceal her ankles. Is careful not to spare Antony a glance for the rest of the night.

—

Days later, his arm brushes against hers as he leans across the table for more wine and her mind floods with images of what a more deliberate touch from him might achieve. That night her sleep is stopped not by horrors from the past but pleasures to come. She rehearses telling him the truth. Or pretending a miracle. Or pouring strong wine down his throat until he cannot tell the difference between man or woman. Or, oh, she knows well some carnal acts that would not require her to reveal herself, but even in her fevered mind such attentions only increase her desire to have him know her fully.

When finally she sleeps she dreams of Randulf on the banks of the Rhine, both of them naked in the mud and the reeds. They kiss and writhe and bite, and as she is about to reach the moment of ecstasy she wakes.

Randulf warned her of this. It is better not to know and so be unable to imagine. To want.

You holy fool, she hears God scoff. *As though the Bible has not been telling you this from the very first!*

But my Lord, she says, if it is so dangerous to know why begin the telling at all? Why make the fruit if not for us to eat?

Brother Antony by her side under the pine. Her feet tucked carefully beneath her, her robe arranged so that nothing but the tips of her fingers are exposed to the air. Her companion takes no such care; sits lazily with his back to the trunk, his legs stretched in front. The tops of his feet dark as the earth, his calves bursts of white light, drawing her gaze.

He is talking of the attack on his home village, how the invaders left bodies in the open to be picked at by birds, torn at by dogs. Anyone attempting to retrieve their dead would quickly join them. He would like to know why it is God made our bodies so that, once the soul is gone, they stink and leak and swell and burst. The abbot at his previous monastery told him it was to remind the living that the flesh is unimportant, that the soul is all. But if the dead flesh is unimportant, why make it draw attention so? Why not make it dissolve like salt in a warm bath?

As though flesh still animated with the breath of God does not draw attention! As if his bared legs do not produce more heat than the midday sun!

'Brother John, you are wiser by far than any man I've known. Why is it, tell me, that God has made us so?'

'You flatter me,' she says, thinking flatter me flatten me sink into me like a warm bath and dissolve me. 'And in doing so you insult our Lord, brother. His creation is perfect, and if we do not see that the fault is in us.'

Antony begs forgiveness. He pouts like a child trying not to cry.

You wicked hypocrite, she thinks. You shame him for his questions while you defile him in your mind.

She could leave. Her reputation is such that she could find work in any of the schools in Athens, perhaps even Alexandria. She hears Brother Theodore muttering about George Constantine, spikily quoting Amma Matrona in the desert: *We carry ourselves wherever we go and cannot escape temptation by flight.*

Brother Antony comes alone in the full heat of day to bring her new wine from the community's vineyards and she cannot tear her gaze from his long, gently tapered fingers as he places the jug on her table. She closes her eyes to pray for strength but finds all she can repeat in her mind is his name, the way she might chant it if those hands were to find their way under her robes. *Antony Antony Antony* she thinks or prays or yearns and then he is touching her arm, asking if she is well. Perhaps the sun has affected her. Perhaps he can assist her inside.

She opens her eyes and God shows her the man's hands as they would appear to his namesake and blessed revulsion evicts her lust. A man worthy of St Antony's name should be sun-darkened and work-roughened. His fingers burred and callused, bent and broken. This smooth-skinned, lazy, decadent imitator is a disgrace to his name.

'I thank you for your gift but cannot use it,' she tells him. 'God has instructed me to drink only water from this day on.'

Disappointment crosses his face. 'You are truly blessed to have God speak to you so directly, Brother John.'

'I will pray for you to receive such guidance, Brother Antony,' she says and does, but God has his own plans and Antony continues to come to her table earlier than the others and leave later. He continues to drink wine until his cheeks are fever red, his lips the exact shade and wetness as they appear in her dreams.

He comes to her as she works alone at the table under the window. Sits close so she can't help but breathe his apple scent, can't help but know the weight of his thigh against hers, the sharp promise of his elbow.

'You will cause the ink to smudge,' she says and he walks outside, lies beneath the stone pine where she can't help but see him.

He looks up at her as though it hurts him to be there without her.

She stands, sits, clenches her fists between her thighs.

This is what the bird feels the moment before it takes flight.

Abba comes to her hut. They sit across from each other at her table, whose surface is scattered with parchment and ink pots and blades and pens, wax tablets and stripped-off covers.

'I must apologise for not having visited you since your earliest days with us, Brother John,' he says. 'I have been remiss.'

'Not at all, Abba. You have always made yourself available to consult and a more gracious father I could not imagine.'

He flicks the compliment away with his hand. 'I spend so much of my time attending to the wellbeing of a very few in our community. Those among us who struggle the most in their communion or their commitment. I have never considered you among their number. Of course I heard rumours over the years. You know the kinds of things people like to whisper. He loves wine more than God. Craves adoration more than salvation. Petty things and none to threaten your greater reputation as a scholar and scribe. Nothing to alter my view of you as pious. As chaste.'

'I am glad to hear it, Abba. I do not claim to be perfect, as no man is, but my piety is heartfelt, as is my chastity.'

He sighs. 'Of late I have heard tales that disturb me. The detail is unimportant. Scurrilous and unfounded, I'm sure. There is something there, though.' He taps his fingers, clawed like a crone, on a parchment she has this morning finished scraping clear. 'A *particular friendship* is how the Benedictines put it, I believe. While we do not forbid such things here on principal, there are times when it becomes evident that a bond is of a nature that contradicts our mission, that threatens the souls of both.'

'Abba, I assure you—'

'Do you know of Anastasia the Patrician?'

'No, Abba.'

'She is revered in our tradition. Sainted. A noblewoman sought out by the great Justinian as a concubine. Being a godly woman Anastasia fled the court rather than lay with him. She travelled to the desert, to Scetis, and there, Abba Daniel seeing her piety and commitment, allowed her to dress as a monk so long as she behaved as one. And so she lived in solitude and service for twenty-eight years, and only after her death did Daniel reveal that this beloved brother had once been a pitiful woman.'

She does not respond. His words are drums of war and it is all she can do to remain seated.

'I, in my imperfection, that is to say humanity, thought the example Abba Daniel set was in following the words of sainted Jerome: *A woman who wishes to serve Christ more in the world will cease to be a woman and will be called man.* On returning to the chronicle I saw my error. It tells us, you see, that having admitted Anastasia to the community Abba Daniel returned to see her every week. He allowed the woman to prove the words of Jerome but he did not leave her alone to do so. He did not leave her alone with temptation. Did not abandon her to her nature.'

Abba stands, rests his hand on the top of her untonsured head. 'I have asked God to forgive me my dereliction of duty.

I hope you will do the same, daughter. And you may, of course, be assured of my scrupulous attentiveness from this point forward.'

He leaves and she breathes deep, is overcome with the stench of her femaleness. It has been swelling and ripening all this time, polluting the very air around her. Perhaps Abba has known her from the start, but with the years she has become complacent. Has worn the robe of a monk while beneath it her body, cow-like, signals that it is ready for mounting and Antony—dear Lord, protect us both—is more bull than any man she has known.

THE LADDER

SHE HACKS OFF the hair Abba touched. A tonsure, all the better for its repellent roughness. She replaces her old cloth bindings with stiff strips of raw linen, adds two extra shifts over the top as well as a cowl and hood for when she must leave the hut. At night, she sleeps as at Fulda, fully dressed save for her sandals.

Her daily serve of goat cheese—sticky and rich as would be expected coming from those vigorous and wanton animals—is surrendered to the common stores and she lets it be known she will not accept offerings of fish, meat or fruit from visitors. A portion of bread and a little salt and water sustained St Antony in the desert and will be more than enough to sustain her here, in her cool and comfortable house in the valley.

Taking only one small meal a day allows her to easily resume the work and prayer routine of Fulda. Although there are no bells to mark time and a sun that moves as though it is a fat and lazy relation of the one she knew back home, the rhythms of the Benedictine day are deep within her bones, sing each change of hour in her blood.

Abba comes not weekly but daily in the hour before the evening meal. She kneels with him beneath the stone pine and they pray together, only ending their devotions when the first visitors arrive. Abba never stays for the feast, but always asks the next day how each of the men is faring. He mentions them by name and it is a sharp stick in her side that the only man he must ask after every day is Brother Antony.

After a month the wisdom of the desert saints is affirmed as her body becomes as it must be: the site of necessary tasks and nothing more. Even these things require less effort as time passes and her body produces less waste, her breasts shrink, her monthly bleed stops.

She hears her visitors talking among themselves, noting that Brother John grows paler, thinner, that his beardless cheeks sink under those sharp northern cheekbones. They must watch he does not become so pious that he will leave them for the life of a true ascetic.

Abba comes less often, though he somehow always knows who has visited and for how long they stayed. When he asks after Brother Antony now she barely notices. He is one among many she is blessed to give sustenance at her table.

The more serious and withdrawn she becomes, the more adoring the attention she receives. Everyone know ascetics are closer to God.

It is amusing, though she has no heart for laughter these days. Her mind soars higher the more she unbinds it from her flesh, and the more she does this, the more the clever and holy men of Athens burn for her.

It doesn't matter. They don't matter. Her mind is God's tool and she will never again keep Him from wielding it fully.

Abba comes early one morning in the company of another man, a book dealer from Alexandria. The dealer wants a translation of a recently discovered text from one of the desert fathers and as many copies as she can make of the original and the translation by spring. 'When I return,' he says, 'I will bring enough gold for you to buy this valley. Perhaps the whole city.'

She has no need for wealth, gives most of her earnings to Abba to spend on the community as he likes. A little she keeps in a pouch beneath her mattress in case of earthquake, plague, war. Revelation.

It is not the promise of gold, then, that keeps her riveted to her desk long past the hour when the locals are accustomed to seeing their beloved Brother John climb the mountain. Not anticipation of riches that leads her to come late to her own feasts and retire early, leaving her visitors to yearn loudly outside of her hut, equally admiring and resentful of the spiritual commitment of their previously convivial brother.

It is—ah, Randulf would not be surprised—the text itself. *The Ladder of Divine Ascent*, a work by St John of Sinai, a father she has never known.

God belongs to all (she reads and feels and knows) *just as the diffusion of light, the sight of the sun, and the changes of the weather are for all alike; there is no respect of persons with God.*

Her mind is, indeed, as he describes: *A greedy kitchen dog addicted to barking and can only be brought to heel through great toil.*

She must, of course, *renounce all things, despise all things, deride all things. Must become as a babe who has no appetite, no stomach, no body on fire.*

She reads the *Ladder* through once, then again and again. She copies a chapter at a time onto newly scraped parchment. Will not move on to the next until she has embodied each.

To live on bread and water she has already mastered. To stay on her feet all night takes a month of practice. Telling Antony he must only visit if he, too, commits to the ladder is easy. Sending him away when he arrives round-eyed and apple-scented, urging her to walk with him to the vineyards or sit a while beneath the pine, these things are more difficult than mortification of her stomach, of going without sleep for nights on end. Finally she tells him he must not come at all and he falls to his knees, clings to the hem of her robe.

'I cannot be without you,' he says, and merely the drag of his fingers on her clothing awakes sensations she was certain she had starved to death.

'St John instructs us that when the fruit is not present we have no desire to eat it.'

He looks up at her, his face glistening with tears. 'You do desire me then? It is not my imaginings?'

'It is a metaphor, Brother Antony. I seek detachment from all things and it is simpler when—'

'I am not a thing. I am your friend.'

'A monk has no friends save the angels.'

She shakes him from her robe, closes her door and ears. Still that night the dream demons come and make metaphor literal. Antony eats of her fruit until his chin drips with its juice. She wakes as her own deceitful hands bring her body to the place it has not reached since Marseille. She shudders and cries with relief then despair.

—

At any point on the ladder, a man may fall. There is no restoration to the last point reached. He must start over and so she does: nights on her feet, salt and bread, a very little water. Mortification of flesh until it forgets there is any other way of being.

Antony surprises her as she tends the chickens. He has prayed on it for forty days and is clearer than ever that God wants the two of them to be in communion. He is an egg tapestried with cracks. She could break him open with a touch.

She walks away without speaking. He seizes her arm and she turns and strikes him hard enough to force him back, then continues on her way. He trails her to the hut, weeping. Stays weeping for hours outside of her closed door.

Do not cease to picture the dark abyss and the unsympathetic inexorable Judge, the bottomless pit of subterranean flame, the narrow descents to the awful underground chambers.

It is easy to picture and in doing so to feel, as one must, *great terror.* She keeps her eyes closed so as to better imagine that endless plummet.

No. Not endless, the plummet, though when you reach the bottom you wish it were.

Skin and hair burn fast and the smell is that of the farmyard after a heifer has dropped in birthing.

RAPTURE

The fat is loud, spits as though in a pan; the muscles twist and pop. You curse the strength and thickness of your bones as they feed the relentless flames. Still more hardy are the lungs, the throat, the tongue. Built sturdy to allow your screams to give warning to those above still able to hear.

'Brother John, it is only that we worry,' Abba calls from outside her hut. 'You scream so that even the brothers on the hill are alarmed. I would pray with you, brother. I ask only for this.'

The motherless girl howls with a wanting so vicious it may split her like a boar.

The hungry child insists God will forgive her for accepting comfort from these well-intentioned but soft and self-deceiving men.

But you *cannot stone the dogs of sensuality with bread* and so the door remains barred and her suffering goes on and it is a blessing to have it hurt as this is the only way to incorruptible chastity.

It is impossible to spend a day devoutly unless we regard it as the last of our life.

It is impossible to spend a day devoutly unless we regard it as the last of our life.

It is impossible to spend a day devoutly unless we regard it as the last of our life.

It is impossible to spend a day devoutly unless we regard it as the last of our life.

It is impossible to spend a day devoutly unless we regard it as the last of our life.

Abba calls for Brother John to come out and the monk writes, *It is not time to bring the spades*, and pushes the scrap of parchment beneath the door, and after a moment Abba says, 'Thanks and glory to God and to Saint Anastasia for her intercession. I will leave our beloved seeker in Your hands.'

Men come and they call to Brother John and there is no answer, for there is nobody of that name here. Only God and the saints know the name of this monk. Only God and the saints will be heard and answered.

THIRTY-THREE

THE ALEXANDRIAN DEALER returns in the spring and gives her a heavy purse for the copies and translation of the work that has saved her soul and restored her vocation. He asks for more of the same, plus copies of this and that *vita*, but she is uninterested despite the riches offered. As her body has stopped craving meat and wine and sex, so too has her mind stopped craving the words of others. With the lack of desire comes a stillness, and within the stillness her own thoughts take deep root and grow.

She calls for novices to run to the city and buy her parchment and ink and then to take her finished texts to this or that scholar. She refuses visitors still, but welcomes written messages. She reads them—*such genius, clear brilliance, wasted in this hermitage, all the gold in the empire*—then scrapes the parchment clean. She writes as long as the light allows, sleeps long and dreamless through the dark.

A scroll wafting sea salt and soil comes addressed to Brother John. The seal is that of Abbot Hatto of Fulda Abbey.

> *My dear Brother John,*
> *After long years of prayerful seeking we lately received word of your place among an Hellenic brotherhood. Be assured we do not write to demand restitution for your theft of church property, that property being yourself. It is true our hearts were greatly saddened by your absconding as we lay on our sick beds. Brother Randulf, on his return to us, told of his attempt to find and restore you to your rightful place. His despair at failing in his mission was grave and for some time his brothers feared for his body and soul. With God's grace he recovered and resumed his vital work for us and was at this godly work when he was taken from this world by vile banditry. This black news reached us in near time to that of your place in Athens as a scholar and scribe of some fame, and so it is that we grieve the loss of one wandering sheep and rejoice in knowing another is alive and flourishing.*
>
> *Having consulted with the obedientiaries and prayed at great length God has led us to* Matthew 5:14–15, *and so it is that we excuse your debt to our house and give blessing for you to follow your calling to serve God in the world. I ask that you continue*

to remember and pray for your forever brothers in Fulda and for the soul of our lost Brother Randulf who tried so valiantly to bring you home.

For the first time in months, she leaves the hut, walks across the valley and makes her way to the top of the mountain. The sky is perfectly blue, perfectly clear. Why should it not be? Randulf had not died this moment, or even this day. And if he had, so what? God cannot turn the world dark every time a man dies. We would never see light at all. Still. The brightness of the day seems a terrible insult. If she had God's ear the way the men of Athens said she did, the whole of Christendom would be breathing ashes and weeping blood.

The bathhouse servants appear alarmed to see the filth-encrusted Brother John lurching towards them. One tells the other to fetch Abba and she tells them to stay where they are. The stone has rolled from the mouth of the tomb. There is a gold coin for each if she remains undisturbed. Two gold coins if they can find for her clean robes and new sandals, a knife to cut her hair.

The water is warm and fragrant, it holds her like a mother. Her bones jut the way they did when she arrived in Athens, but beneath the months of dirt her skin is soft as a newborn babe—except for her feet, which have grown their own sole leather, and her knees, which are hard as a camel's.

Eight years she has lived without Randulf and she cannot know how much of that time he was already gone from the earth. It should not matter, then, this news. It changes nothing.

And yet. And yet.

There is no one left on this earth who knows who she once was. Who she is.

When she saw the last person who would ever call her Agnes she was twenty-five years old and now she is thirty-three. She has lived twice as long as her mother and half as long as her father. She is the age of Hild when she found God and her life truly began. The age of Christ at his death, which was also his becoming.

She is thirty-three years old and no one in this world knows her, and God, who does, has sent her a message by way of his servant in Fulda.

You are the light of the world, he has said. *A city that is set on a hill cannot be hid. Neither do men light a candle and put it under a bushel, but on a candlestick, and it gives light unto all that are in the house.*

She is alone and undivided, clean and hunger-less and strong. She is God's brightest candle and He is calling her out of this sheltered valley so she may give light to all in His lately darkening house.

SHE TAUGHT THE LIBERAL
ARTS AND HAD GREAT
MASTERS AMONG HER
STUDENTS AND AUDIENCE

(850-855)

MADE FOR EACH OTHER

THE LETTER FROM Abbot Hatto releasing her from her vows and a letter of introduction and commendation from Abba in Athens see her welcomed into the guesthouse of the Schola Greca, established in Rome by those great men forced to flee their homeland due to the madness of the iconoclasts. For a month she wanders the city, learning its paths and its perils. In Athens, the Christians turned ancient temples into churches; here they've been torn apart for building materials, their remaining nooks turned into latrines, their arches display cases for whores or cook stations for street peddlers.

She visits the amphitheatre where Ignatius was ground to grain by wild beasts, his blood soaking into earth already well-watered by centuries of blood sport, and though this killing field is crammed with people, not a one of them is thinking of the martyrs or the emperors who condemned them. Here, now, children of God are bent double, ropes around their middles, dragging chunks of stone to make room for tents and lean-tos. They balance stacks of bricks on their heads, tip them into piles outside the diminishing walls, and others take them up, cart them to the new building they're erecting out of these ancient discards. Worker ants crisscross the centre circle that once smelt of innards and gizzards and now festers with the stench of kilns burning marble into lime to meet the needs of construction.

Pilgrims wash through, chanting and bowing and telling each other stories of the past, theirs and Rome's. For most who live here, though, the Eternal City only exists in this moment. What came before is irrelevant except insofar as shreds and threads can be used to make the present more powerful and real.

She takes it all in, thinks, We are made for each other, Rome and me.

At the Schola Greca she gives a public lecture on *The Ladder of Divine Ascent* and afterwards is kept for hours by students and masters of the school asking questions about the text, her translations, her time in Athens. The following day she receives invitations to speak at the scholas Saxonum, Francium and

Frisian. Within ten days suitors from every school in Rome have visited to heap praise and promises of glory at her feet if only she will join their institution. In the place she already calls home, the Schola Greca, she is offered the position Professor of Theology, given freedom to create the curriculum, to hire and oversee teachers, and—most valuable of all to she whose body sweats and creases and pains beneath her straps and robes—a house of her own with a private bath and garden, right there behind the school on the Aventine Hill.

There are more churches on this one hill than in the entire city of Mainz, and as she walks past them each day after Prime and before her first lecture—past her schola's own church of Santa Maria, then churches for St Sabina, St Alessio, St Giorgio in Velabro, St Saba, St Prisca, St Ballina—she thinks of the English Priest, who believed their little city with its little cathedral could be mistaken for Rome, and she grieves for him that he did not know how inglorious his version of glory was.

Her first lecture as Professor of Theology is to a small room of eager students. Her second is moved to a larger space so fellow professors may attend as well as invited guests from beyond the school. Soon, the *primicerius* asks that Brother John conduct a public lecture once a week. Scholars from all over Rome arrive early to ensure entry; some send servants or pay messengers to stand for hours to hold their place.

'It is a rare teacher who compels students to stay awake throughout the lesson,' says the *primicerius*. 'I have never met one who manages, as you do, to arouse them to a state of higher wakefulness still.'

It helps, she knows, that her skin has been leathered by years of Athenian sun, the planes of her face carved sexless by years of bare living, her voice scratched hoarse by deprivation and strain. She is, to her students and the increasing number of non-studious attendees, the very image of a revered desert father, though scrubbed clean and speaking a language they can understand. She is a way into the wisdom of the great Hermetics without having to travel beyond the city nor withstand the stench of an unwashed, worm-infested body. She offers the knowledge of the finest monastic scholars without the impenetrable grammar and unbearable dourness.

But there is this too: the most famed theological teachers and orators of Rome, she discovers, are more concerned with politics than God, with acquiring power in the earthly church than a place in heaven. Taxes, tithes, bishoprics and papal powers. These are the things occupying the minds of Roman Christians. Brother John is provocative in his refusal to engage with the issues of the day. His lectures are about the soul, the trinity, the intercessions of saints, and to hear him, people say, is to know what it was to hear Jesus of Nazareth preach in Galilee.

Sometimes men are moved to tears by her words, and if they are rich or important or patient enough these men find their way to the front of the hall and position themselves so their tears fall at her feet. They gaze up at her with eyes and mouths wet and hungry and she thinks of Antony in Athens, and also of Agnes in Mainz. A commonplace tragedy: the student so greedy he will swallow whatever the teacher offers. The teacher so in love with his own greatness he believes a student's body—which is to say soul—a fair salary.

She avoids meeting eyes with the would-be disciples, refuses private meetings altogether. Pride, like lust, is a lion that cannot be slayed, only starved. She crams her waking hours with prayers: performs the offices with her fellows at the schola and always, if she is not teaching or writing, she is silently reciting: *Lord Jesus Christ, Son of God, have mercy on me, a sinner.*

At the close of each lecture or class, when human devotion threatens to unleash the beast in her heart, she prostrates herself beneath the fat eastern cross nailed to the wall, prays: Lord, help this sinner remember she is nothing but a vessel for your word. Fame is not real. Adoration is not real. The Schola Greca is not real. Rome is not real. Brother John is not real. Agnes is not real. I am, as we all are, a soul waiting to be released into heaven, and my work has value only in that it may help light the path for others.

Usually while she prays thus the room behind her empties, even the most fervent of devotees eventually chased out by her assistants: four men chosen for their ability to glare in ways that make the obscenely rich and powerful feel like scolded children. On this day, though, twenty-two months after her appointment to the schola, she says, *Amen*, and lifts her head and opens her eyes not to an empty hall but to a man dressed in the full livery of the papal household.

Our Holiness Pope Leo IV requests Brother John's presence at the Lateran Palace this evening after Vespers.

THE BASILISK SLAYER

THE LATERAN PALACE. A mess of penitents and supplicants in front of the gate. A guard views her letter of invitation, calls on his fellows to assist in holding back the crowd as he admits her. Another guard appears and leads her across a courtyard, past a portico where nuns in blue stack bags of grain for the hungry waiting outside. On the far side of that building is another gate leading onto another courtyard, past several more small buildings, through a third gate behind which a bronze she-wolf feeds two babes from her swollen teats. She would like to pause and examine the sculpture which stands almost as tall as her, would like to know the reason for such a shockingly pagan image in this holiest of places, but her guide hurries her towards yet another gate, after which he stops still, directs her to go alone down a covered passage tiled with mosaic swirls the colour of the morning sky. At the end there is a set of doors, dark rough-hewn wood reaching almost as high as the roof. The liveried attendant waiting there raps with his staff and after a moment the doors swing open and she is urged forward into the Great Hall.

The hall is vast and cool, lit dimly by candles hung high on the wall, as though it is still the time of Constantine. As though the doomed adulteress Fausta will any moment sweep across this field of marble and offer her a goblet of wine. But there is no one here, living or dead. Only her, small as a child in this space built for giants.

On the wall to her left hangs the largest map she has seen. She examines it as long as the attendant who appears from the ether allows, which is mere seconds but long enough for a new space in her to form and immediately begin complaining of its emptiness. Behold how much there is of this world and how very little of it you have known, it sings.

In the papal apartments richly coloured Byzantium carpets and gold-threaded tapestries line the floors and walls. Silver chalices and basins flash atop hardwood chests. Emeralds, rubies and diamonds wink at her from all. In the third room of the apartment she is presented to the tiny, white-haired man on a throne twice her height, covered in gold and lined with purple satin. They say this man once slayed a basilisk terrorising St Lucia's church. He used prayer rather than sword, but still she expected someone larger and more fierce.

She bends her knee and kisses his slipper, as the attendant said she must. The slipper is whiter than Athenian limestone and smells like nothing and she wonders if it was placed clean on his foot after he was seated or if the floors here are kept pristine enough that not a shadow of filth can transfer.

Randulf, she thinks, would enjoy this place, this man. Raised a Benedictine, now living like Nero.

She has barely thought of Randulf in her time here, cannot allow his memory to distract her now. The Pope's chamberlain is offering her wine and the Holy Father himself is speaking to her about the lecture she gave that morning. He was moved, he is saying. He was humbled. He was thrilled. He only hoped the presence of his considerable retinue was not a distraction.

'Not at all, Holy Father,' she says. 'I did not notice you were there.'

An attendant gasps. Leo blinks. Shadow flames dance on the wall behind his head.

'Ah!' the Pope says at last. 'Listen, my children, to this true messenger of the Lord who is without self when conducting his sacred task! Just when I had almost given up hope of finding a single man in this great city who shares my own commitment to a perfect, Christlike humility.'

—

Leo summons her again the following day. She bends, kisses, stands while he remains seated above her. He tells her of the history of the Schola Greca as if she does not live and work there, then lectures her on the iconoclastic crisis as if she had not come to Rome from eight years in the east, had not broken bread with priests whose churches had been limewashed and defaced, had not seen in Athens the repainted frescoes, the gloriously restored saints.

When he says, 'Why do they call you "the English"?' she wants to say, *You tell me.*

'My father hailed from Wessex, Your Holiness, and I am named for him.'

'You are not English, though?'

'I am a Frank, Your Holiness. Raised in the Archbishopric of Mainz.'

And he is off again with a lecture about the conversion of the Franks. She tries to imagine him in his monastic days. The vow of silence like an infestation of worms in his blood.

Finally he segues into his recent dealings with the emperor, a Frank like her—'*Your Lothar,*' he calls him.

The name raises the dead. All those split-faced, maggot-gnawed, crow-eaten boys scattered across Burgundy and beyond. At once their stench overpowers the sweet wafting incense. Their too-soon forgotten bones clatter against the gold-embossed walls.

Leo's speechifying outlasts the protestations of the dead and here she is still, in this shining fragrant room, hearing how old Lothar thrives thanks to papal blessing—which is to say, of course, God's grace, and in recognition of this grace, he, Lothar, blesses Rome with some of the fruits of his success.

The Pope wants to know what Brother John has heard of his predecessor, Sergius II. Before she can answer he says, 'I wish I could say the stories were untrue. It was a dark time for us all.'

The stories she has heard, and which she is grateful not to be asked to repeat, are many: that Sergius and his brother grew fat and rich by selling off bishoprics and land titles to the highest bidder; that the building works contracted to cover their swindle were done cheaply, resulting in collapses and disaster; that having been warned of an imminent attack by the Saracens he raised his hands to heaven and said, *God will protect*; that safe within the city walls he feasted on roast pig and Sicilian wine while more than ten thousand marauders made easy work of every church and home outside of those walls; that he was in bed, moaning over the gout that would soon kill him, while St Peter's and St Paul's Outside the Walls were desecrated, every reliquary smashed open, sacred relics used as obscene props, even the walls and doors stripped of their silver.

'I will never forget,' Leo is saying, 'that you foreigners were among the few who came out to defend our sacred heritage. All these fine men of the scholas—Saxon, Frisian, you

Franks—taking on the invaders, staunch with the knowledge that learning and faith are stronger than steel.'

He speaks as though those poor students rushed willingly to their deaths. As though they were not stuck outside the walls in direct way of the marauders. As though they were not—every clever, faithful one of them—slaughtered by actual steel weapons while the Roman Army and Papal Guard watched from a safe and fortified distance.

Never mind all that; Leo is back to the terrible shame of the desecrated and robbed churches. He has, of course, made it a priority to restore them to their former glory. Himself all alone replacing the sacred riches of centuries! He recites them for her like a poem he has practised every night since childhood:

'For Peter's confessio I gave:
fine silver railings weighing eight hundred pounds
four silver-gilt panels for the steps
and two lambs, silver, too, together weighing forty-four pounds
and porphyry crowns decorated in fine gold
each with twelve dolphins and Peter's holy name
Also ten fine silver arches decorated with gold interweave
Liturgical gifts, too,
of course of course you will have heard perhaps seen
my crucifix
the crucifix of wondrous size of fine silver-gilt and with jacinth jewels and one other large pearl

seventy-seven pounds it weighs!

My crucifix.'

She tells him she visits the basilica often and has wept at its beauty, unknowing it was he who was responsible. None of this is true. It is a long, dusty walk to St Peter's from Aventine Hill and the streets surrounding the church heave with construction work; if she had wept on her one visit it would have been at the stink of pilgrims and clamour of the guides shouting about the generosity of Leo IV.

The Pope sniffs, asks if she knows of the naval campaign he launched immediately after being raised to the throne. Again, he forges on without waiting for reply. Tells how he mobilised the Roman forces and worked with Naples, Amalfi and Gaeta to beat back the repeated attempts of the Saracens to occupy these lands.

'It is said,' she risks, 'that your own prayers made all the difference, Holy Father. That God heard your entreaties and raised a mighty storm that favoured our men and secured the victory.'

Leo narrows his eyes at the interruption but she can see he is pleased. A man as desperate to appear humble as he is for people to know his glory.

His primary task since, he continues, has been to restore the old Aurelian wall and rebuild the towers felled by the invaders or crumbled through neglect.

Again she speaks without invitation. 'More than restored, Your Holiness. The wall you build for us extends around St Peter's and the Vatican, does it not? As it surely always should have.'

He glowers and glows at once. 'No longer will enemies of God be allowed to swing their way into the most sacred places and smash and take whatever they like!' His frail, silk-swathed arms wave in what she assumes is his impression of dastardly church-smashing but which reminds her of nothing so much as a Mainz market wife shooing flies from her wares.

'Enough,' he says sharply, as if she has been wasting his time. 'My valet will furnish you with the details.'

He stands, descends the steps from his throne, offers his hands for her to kiss, swishes out of a door that has appeared only this moment in the back wall of the room.

The door disappears into the wall again. A liveried man takes her arm and ushers her out the way she entered. He speaks as fast as he walks. She is alone, blinking beneath the setting Roman sun, before she understands she is to join the Holy Father at the consecration of his wall the following week.

On 27 June 852 Agnes of Mainz, Frankish daughter of an English priest and a German pagan, joins Pope Leo IV and his cardinals, bishops, priests and deacons at the Porta San Pellegrino. Barefoot and with ash-smeared foreheads they process around the wall, pausing to bless each gate along the way.

Men captured at the Battle of Ostia were forced to build this wall. Their sweat and blood is in its mortar. It was a mercy, Father Leo says, to bind them in iron so they could learn of the true God and His ineffable pity. A mercy to spare them from living idly by giving them good work to do. A mercy to allow them to redeem their lives on earth and perhaps even their souls.

Only half of them were shown this apparent mercy, she knows, the others left hanging from trees on the road to Rome until they were no longer recognisable as men. Did these poor lost strangers know St Paul was martyred on that same road? Did the men hoisting the ropes—the Christian soldiers of Rome—know?

At each new gate Leo says a prayer for the city founded with God's assistance. May it remain safe from His wrath. May it triumph always over the enemies who have inspired its construction.

Sweat, or perhaps the holy water flicked about by the cardinals, has turned the ash on her forehead to mud. It irritates her skin and threatens to blind her eyes.

Afterwards, Leo commands her to come to the Lateran Palace the following morning. Now that this project is finished he has many new plans he wishes to discuss.

'Forgive me, Your Holiness. My students will be expecting—'

'Your students must be content with whichever man has been found to replace you. I will see you after Lauds.'

He walks ahead, surrounded by men in robes almost as long as his. An aide tells her the Holy Father wishes Brother John to join his staff. A room in the palace is being prepared. She should send her belongings before she leaves the schola in the morning.

'Brother,' she pleads, 'I am a teacher. I have nothing to offer the palace.'

The man shakes his head. 'The Holy Father is gone. No need to pretend humility.'

'I pretend nothing. My calling is to teach.'

'Do you not believe,' the man says, leaning in as though he might kiss her, might bite her nose, 'that our Lord handed the apostle Peter the keys of the kingdom of heaven and did grant him the pontificate of binding and loosing and that this grant is the very same one that has been delivered to our Holy Father Leo IV?'

She would like to spit in his eye. This tiny man made big by the gold braid on his shoulders. This weak man wielding an impossible question as a weapon.

'I do, of course.'

'Your calling, then, *John the English*, is that which he calls you to. Yes?'

She nods. It is done.

RAPTURE

—

Alone in her little house for the last time she picks gravel from the torn flesh of her feet and weeps at her stupidity and vanity. She had no need to flatter Leo so. He would have forgotten clever Brother John after one dull meeting, left her to continue teaching until old age took her. Her pride, that lion, never dead only sleeping. And lightly at that.

RENEWED AND REVIVIFIED

LEO'S TITLES ARE many: Pontifex Maximus, Romanus Pontifex, Primate of the Bishops of the Church, Patriarch of Rome, Vicar of Rome, Apostolic Lord, Servant of the Servants of God. After a few days as a notary in his office, she adds silently: chief landholder, property manager, head grocer and dispensator of Rome. How do other cities operate, she wonders, without the Pope to provide housing for the masses, arrange repairs to public buildings, fund education, build and maintain the aqueducts and ensure grain and meat supply? Surely this is not what Jesus intended for the heirs of St Peter?

Though in reality, she sees, such work is done by the Pope in name only. The contracts and titles and registers, the accounts of incoming earnings (the Patrimony of St Peter consisting of vast swathes of land on every part of the known earth, but particularly here in Italy where the weekly earnings from four estates alone outstrip what Fulda Abbey earns in a year) and the payment of bills and honorariums are all done by clerics and notaries and overseen by the *vestiarius*. It is dull, painstaking work provoking the same existential boredom and physical aches she suffered in her earliest days in the Fulda scriptorium. It is the greatest honour, of course, to be doing it.

Though stinking with humanity within almost as without, the Lateran Palace is a cold and solitary place. The halls rustle with whispered schemes she is never close enough to hear properly. If an eye meets yours in here you cannot be sure it did not come sideways. She works, she prays, she sleeps, she tries to understand God's intention in placing her here, reminds herself His will is not hers to know, only to accept.

A crate of wine for the papal cellars has arrived from some northern duke and it is her task to compose a letter that will both thank him sincerely and make clear that the wine is no substitute for the rent he owes. She wonders how she might get the letter wrong in a way which will displease Leo enough that he releases her back to the schola but not so much she is sent to the dungeons. Although the dungeons may not be so bad. At least there she will not have to hear her fellow notaries muttering and throat-clearing all day long.

'Brother John, the Frankish Englishman.' As though she has conjured him, Leo stands before her, flanked by his favoured cardinals, who are themselves flanked by senior clerics.

She turns from her desk, kneels, kisses the ring on the hand he offers. 'Your Holiness.' She hopes he will tell her to stand; her knees have never recovered from the months she spent on them in Athens and the floor in this room is particularly cold and hard.

He withdraws his hand and speaks over the top of her head. 'This Gottschalk. Your brother at Fulda.'

Gottschalk. The child oblate Randulf spoke about with such longing. The man who won his freedom only to have it taken away on appeal.

'Brother Gottschalk left before I—'

A staff slams down near her left foot. One of the cardinals reminding her that no question has been asked of her. She bows her head lower and Leo goes on.

'He continues to stir up trouble, this brother of yours.'

She says nothing, waits.

Leo says, 'You are aware of his activities?'

'I am aware he was condemned for his heresies at the synod in Quiercy, Holy Father.'

Condemned by the Archbishop of Hincmar, flogged in front of Charles the Bald, forced to burn his own writings, imprisoned within the walls of yet another detested monastery.

'And still he carries on with this double predestination nonsense! He gathers support! I have no end of correspondence from good men of our church wondering if there might be something in what he claims.'

The other men mutter in outrage and she waits, pain spiralling up her thighs, until Leo says, 'A document outlining the church's official response is needed. Something we can send to the misled.'

She waits. The men in front of her shuffle and murmur.

'You will prepare this document, Brother John,' says one of the cardinals.

'Your Eminence, I—'

'You can stand. The Holy Father has gone.'

She rises. Only one cardinal—Prudentius, she believes—remains. 'Your Eminence, I am a mere notary. This is surely a task for—'

'We have consulted masters of the finest schools in Rome on this matter. All agree you have the right combination of theological rigour and elegance of phrasing.'

'The responsibility is too much, Your Eminence.'

'The responsibility is bestowed on you by the Apostolic Lord who acts for God and so cannot be mistaken.'

'Yes, Your Eminence.'

'And be quick with it, brother. Our Holy Father meets with his archbishops next week and must be well prepared.'

Dear Lord, she thinks, when the cardinal has left her. Why must you always take me literally? I hope you will at least clear the rats from the dungeon before I am cast down.

Her first abbot, Hrabanus Maurus, the same man who refused to release Gottschalk and who maintained his rage at the oblate being assigned to a different abbey, has won, twenty years after the young monk attempted to free himself from life in a monastery. It feels a terrible betrayal to Randulf to write a document that vindicates Hrabanus, condemns Gottschalk from the highest throne on earth.

But it is not only a matter of obedience to the Holy Father. Gottschalk *is* wrong about predestination. He must be, or otherwise there are some predestined to die in sin and never know heaven and those who will reach God's side have already been chosen. That cannot be true, for if it is then nothing anyone does on earth—nothing at all—can matter.

She writes as powerfully and clearly as she can. Writes as though her living body and soul depend on it, because they do, they do. Christ suffered for all men so all men may be saved. All of us, predestined only to live in this world, all of us able to secure a place in the next.

Leo and his coterie find her back at her desk in the notaries' office. Again she kneels and kisses his ring. This time he tells her to stand. He tells her how well the document has been received. It is not credited to Brother John, of course, but that is as it should be given that the words were fed to her directly by God.

And therefore attributed to you, Your Holiness, she does not say.

There is a problem, the cardinals gathered around her desk a month or so later, tell her. Although their Holy Father is, everyone knows, a wise, kind and generous man imbued with the glory of God, this is not always evident to the people of Rome. Our Holiness believes that it is because God has marked Brother John out as the great communicator of His kingdom on earth. This has been done in order to free our Holiness for more important work. God has put Brother John here in order to produce the homilies and prayers and speeches of His chosen representative, and it is because he has not done so that the Holy Father's public appearances do not succeed as they should. From now on, Brother John will compose the words that Leo speaks in public and do so in such a way that the people perceive him, Leo, as a great shepherd to his flock, audience for God's will and transmitter of Jesus's touch.

What no one says but is nonetheless perfectly clear is that it will not be enough for her to write sermons and prayers as moving and erudite as those she once gave at the schola. Leo is an old man of thin voice and aristocratic manner. If he ever glowed with the love of Christ or emitted the warmth of a kindly pastor that time is long gone. Words that, spoken by Brother John, might bring senior clerics to tears and make the wealthy and poor alike interrupt their work to send praise to Jesus will fall flat and dull coming from the Pope's mouth.

Leo's speeches and prayers must be grand enough, in other words, to survive his delivery.

She thinks back to meals at Fulda, how the brothers with the dullest affect seemed always to be the ones chosen to read aloud, as though the abbot wanted them all to fall asleep in their soup or be gripped with such existential boredom they stop eating altogether. And yet, every now and then the reading itself was of such brilliance that even the flattest of tones took on resonance, even the dustiest of readers shimmered with erudition and inspiration.

The *Vita Sturmi*, she recalls, was one such text, pulsing with so much life it could animate the man reading it without his effort or even knowledge. When the chronicler describes the wild beasts, naked barbarians and vicious Saxons that Sturmi encountered while founding the Fulda Abbey every man in the refectory with half his wits knew that the battleground described in the *vita* was not the one in which they lived and worked. Even accounting for the clearing of trees and construction of buildings, the wilderness of the *vita* was a spiritual wilderness made vivid for the text. And yet every man in the room, witted or not, felt the racing in his veins. Every one of them, her included, sitting taller, a soldier defending the frontier of heaven itself.

She finds the *vita* in the Lateran library, reads and rereads, taking copious notes until she has it memorised. She repeats the most powerful lines instead of her prayers until their structure and rhythm pulses through her like blood. She writes, has junior notaries who've never spoken so much as their full names out loud perform her texts. Rewrites until the dullest of her assistants seems a leader of men so long as he is speaking her words.

Soon, it is said in Rome and beyond that the Holy Father has been renewed and revivified after the understandable depletion caused by the years of strengthening Rome's defences and restocking its treasures. All this accomplished, Leo IV is now dedicated to bringing the word of God directly to the people. To hear him pray, it is said, is to know what it is to be in the Lord's presence; it is to feel the wings of angels passing rapturously overhead.

THE REAL WORK

LEO COMES TO her desk, surrounded as always by his red-breasted flock of cardinals. 'You remind me very much of another. Anastasius. A brilliant man, educated by the Greeks, like you, a masterful scribe and translator. Flawless biblical commentaries. Oh, how I grieve his loss.' Leo closes his eyes. Says, 'Lord protect and save him.'

The men surrounding Leo repeat the prayer. Only she, who is facing him, can see that Cardinal Vergilius, the Pope's chief adviser, keeps his eyes open. Open and stony.

'Holy Father, forgive my hurrying but we are late, and I am sure, too, that Brother John must be getting on with his work.'

Leo sniffs. 'There are a hundred men here who can do this work. There are few with an intellect and faith like our Brother John. He will join my personal staff. Prudentius, see to it.'

'Congratulations, brother,' Cardinal Prudentius says when Leo and the rest are gone. 'Now you will be where the real work happens.'

'I am honoured, Your Eminence. I pray God allows me to serve the Holy Father as well as my late predecessor Anastasius.'

'Pah! That is a favour to be granted by the devil!'

'Your Eminence?'

'Anastasius is not dead in body but spirit. Brilliant, yes, but also scheming, dishonest, treacherous. Our Lord Pope loved him like a son, made him cardinal priest of St Marcellus, but the arrogance of the man—encouraged by his equally ambitious uncle—knew no bound. He plotted to take the throne from our Holy Father and was exiled. Excommunicated. Dead to our church and lost to Christ.'

'Then I shall pray for his redemption and for God to steer me clear of his path.'

She works now in the lavish room where she first met Leo. When the day is at its peak, there are twelve men in here, though mirrors make them an army. The carpet is so thick each appears half a head shorter—all except Leo himself, who floats on his golden throne, his reflection beaming back at himself over and over and over.

The crisis of the moment: the Archbishop of Ravenna has seized papal property for himself. Cardinal Prudentius recommends an armed party be sent to reclaim the property. Cardinal Servius urges caution. Ravenna is under the protection of King Louis, himself under the protection of his father, Emperor Lothar, and no one here when Sergius annoyed the two of them back in '44 should be in a hurry to do so again.

Leo and his advisers reference history the way the brothers of Fulda reference Scripture. Scripture is welcome here too, of course, but words spoken by St Paul eight centuries past cannot compete with a reminder of the Frankish troops massed at the gates threatening to sack the city as brutally as any pack of Northmen.

Yes, the Psalms are known to all here, but so too is the knowledge that the last Leo to sit on this throne was dragged to the ground during a sacred procession, had his eyes scored out and his tongue near removed. And though St Matthew's gospel is frequently aired, even that cannot calm the fear that shivers through the room when mention is made of the revenge taken upon the inner circle of Antipope Constantine II. Every man in this room has imagined himself hounded through the streets of Rome with weights chained to his splintering ankles.

When Hrabanus Maurus found himself on the wrong side of the Carolingian war he had a period of contemplation in a mountain retreat before being made Archbishop of Mainz. When a pope falls foul of the old families of Italy, the Vatican reverts to Nero's pleasure garden and there is no guarantee he will emerge with all his parts or indeed his life.

The real work of the Lateran, then, is existential.

'Lothar is our friend,' Servius declares, after much discussion about the wisdom of appealing to an emperor over a king, of striking against a favoured son of the old Italian nobility or letting it be known the church does not protect its assets. 'We can appeal to him to intervene.'

'He is our friend but he is Louis' father.'

'Nevertheless,' Leo has decided, 'it is right Lothar knows of the avarice and illegality of this little man in Ravenna.'

So it is that emissaries are dispatched to inform the emperor, and the cardinals and Pope enjoy some grapes and cheese, a little more wine and—why not?—a honeyed fig cake.

The emissaries are dispatched from Rome and, soon, from the world. Two good men murdered on the road, throats cut by knives bearing the insignia of the Duke of Emilia, the brother of that thieving archbishop.

Though the cardinals argue long into the night, pausing

only to perform the offices and eat from the platters sent hourly from the kitchens, Leo is adamant there is only one course of action. He will go, himself, to Ravenna. Let the enemies of this office dare to cut down the Bishop of Rome. Let them try and let them see the punishment God delivers.

While he is abroad he may as well take the opportunity to meet with Louis, ask if it is true he intervened personally to save the men condemned to hang for the murder of the papal envoys. Ask too why it is he continues in his patronage of the Bishop of Orte, Arsenius, and his poisonous, ambitious son, Anastasius.

And also! He might just ask this so-called King of Italy if he cares to assist at all in defending Rome against the continued Saracen threat. Or does he believe that Leo, descendant of Peter, fisher of men, should be responsible for protecting the life of every Roman as well as their souls?

The cardinals ooze anxiety and fear, but the discussion is finished. This is what will be.

'I will be gone throughout Easter,' Leo says. 'It cannot be helped. Tonight we will all of us feast for luck. Tomorrow I leave for Ravenna. Prudentius and Vergilius, you will come with me.'

He issues more directives: which cardinal priest will stand in for him on which holy day, which cleric or notary will be responsible for which task during his absence. 'Brother John . . .' he says, and the room holds its collective breath, waiting to see what task he might assign this most junior of attendants, this well-liked but insignificant monk. 'Brother John, you will pray for me and my mission.'

'As we all will, Your Holiness,' says Servius.

Leo flicks his hand. 'Brother John will pray for this mission the way I prayed for the storm that defeated the Saracens. His prayers will carry the angel of the Lord aloft with his sword and bring us back alive and triumphant.'

Dinner is held in the same vast hall where she stood shivering on her first admittance to the palace. Tonight there are ten times as many candles: they blaze from complicated towers running the length and height of the walls. A dozen men gather beneath the map of the known world, talking among themselves, and she wonders if they truly do not wish to examine it in detail or if they are, like her, convinced that to do so would be an error, although she cannot, even to herself, explain why.

The bell—multiple bells, as light and chirping as the birds of Thuringia—ring and the men move to their assigned seats. Four long tables of thirteen arranged in a square. Four blatant forgeries of the last supper. Leo is in the centre of the table which faces the world. The men on either side of him—Vergilius on the left, Prudentius on the right—each appears to think himself the centre. Neither competes for the Pope's attention but rather sits back: Vergilius amused, Prudentius sneering, as other men further along call across the chosen two with their simpering and sycophancy. The men at Leo's table are the most senior, but not his most trusted and loved. Those men are seated where Leo can easily catch their gaze. It soothes and comforts him, she knows, to look up in the midst of a dinner like this and see his greatest friends at the table across from him: Servius, Gregor, Winfrith and, in the very centre, directly across from the Holy Father, Brother John.

There is chanting and praying and, as they eat, a babel of conversation from which scraps of Scripture reach her like windblown ash. God's name in every mouth, yet is any of this His? None of it is biblical, not even the Pope.

Candlelight catches the crosses hanging from every neck, makes the gold shine, the jewels sparkle. Only her own is of plain wood like that Jesus was nailed to. All of us in disguise here, she thinks. Which of us would Christ recognise as his servants, truly?

He recognises *her*, it seems. Leo and his retinue return to Rome after six weeks, safe and satisfied with the outcome of their diplomatic efforts. All praise Brother John for his successful prayer vigil. None, she supposes, believe there was anything special in her prayers. None except Leo, whom she is sure is sincere. 'Your faith is more powerful than any sword,' he says, and she recalls he said the same of the students who resisted the Saracen invasion. The students who were cut to pieces nonetheless.

The following morning, when the bell rings for Terce, she is stopped from leaving with the others. From now on Brother John will sing the offices with Leo and his closest advisers in the Sancta Sanctorum, entered through a door almost hidden in the wall behind the throne.

Before they kneel Leo points to the reliquary, modelled on the Ark of the Covenant—though that ancient sacred object was not, presumably, inlaid with hundreds of jewels. 'You will have heard, I suppose, what it is we hold here?'

'I have, Holy Father, and I am moved and honoured beyond words to be in the presence of wood from the true cross of our Lord Jesus Christ.'

Leo leans in close as, behind him, Vergilius, shockingly, rolls his eyes. 'Not only that,' Leo says, 'but the holy foreskin as well. A gift to the palace from Charles the Great himself. Imagine!'

Praying in the Holy of Holies, shoulder to shoulder with God's chosen representative on earth, she feels nothing save for the pain in her knees.

VALENTINE

'DO YOU KNOW,' says Cardinal Servius, as the two of them puzzle together over a fifth-century scroll alleged to grant a far-off convent to the Bishop of Rome, 'there are many in these halls who refer to you now as Valentine?'

She scans her mental *Liber Pontificalis* for the relevant detail. Valentine was pope for a bare two months thirty years ago. A noble, made Bishop of Rome before he was even a priest. She cannot grasp the comparison. The insult. To Servius she says, 'And they refer to you as the unicorn. Such nonsense these names, no?'

Even as she says it she sees she has indicted herself for crimes unknown. Servius's epithet is, in fact, accurate in its way; like the fabled beast, his only known weakness is the attention of a young virgin. He might be pope himself by now if it were not for the scores of noble daughters he has ruined for all but the convent.

'Indeed,' Servius says. 'These men do not know you at all. Nor do they know our Holy Father.' He smiles for a heartbeat and she sees instantly what those poor young virgins must see the moment before all is lost. 'Any man suggesting that Brother John and Leo IV are lovers should be strangled in his sleep—for stupidity as much as blasphemy.'

The *Liber Pontificalis* has failed her in its scrupulous avoidance of controversy. There is no hint there that Valentine had ascended the throne from between Eugene II's sheets.

'Any man who truly knows how this city works and who knows you, Brother John, understands the real reason you are our Holy Father's favourite.'

She leans closer to the document in front of her. It is terribly written; Latin assembled as if it were Gaelic, the ink fading, the parchment blotched and pin-holed. She knows they are expected to conclude the grant is inarguable. The armed party to claim the property for the Lateran is already on its way.

'Oh, you are clever, of course,' Servius continues. 'But clever men are as common as whores in this city.'

She cannot resist; says, 'We must move in different circles as I have come across neither.'

He chuckles. 'Ah, that's it exactly, though. You move in no circles at all. A lately Hermetic foreigner with no ties to defend, no ecclesiastical or scholarly feuds to continue or resolve. As for whores, well, no one can say you have even once consorted with such since your arrival in Rome, nor do you keep a mistress. Or master, papal or otherwise. And believe me, brother, enquiries have been made.'

'You seem to be suggesting chastity is rare among men who are sworn to it.'

'Oh, I do enjoy you, brother. Yes, yes, let's all pretend half the treasury isn't spent supporting bastards and brothels and the immaculately conceived progeny of nuns.'

'It grows late, Your Eminence, and I would like to complete this task before Nocturnes.'

'What does it matter? You have nowhere to go once your prayers are done. It is this that makes you Leo's pet, Brother John. No family, no loyalties, no risk of scandal or blackmail. You can belong to him entirely.'

'I belong to God,' she says, and Servius smiles again, pats her on the back as though they agree.

All night his words cut through her thoughts: *Believe me, brother, enquiries have been made.*

She hears Randulf in her head: *Rome is not Fulda. It isn't even Mainz.* It is certainly not Athens, that gentle old city, where one can be famous and adored while hiding away in a hut at the base of a mountain. She had thought it God's will that she shine her light more brightly; did not wonder if it might be the devil or her own pride (and what, after all, is the difference?) tempting her here.

This is not Fulda, but Randulf would surely know how to play it, how to cultivate friends and allies in every pocket of the place. He would know at which table to eat plain bread and speak of God's will and at which to suck marrow from bone and joke about whores and wine.

This is not Mainz, but her father would do well here, she's sure. Every night he facilitated factional battles at his table, ruled and influenced without ever seeming to care very much one way or the other. The men did not love him, she understands now, but they relied on him. Needed him.

She needs him. Them. Someone.

She is a brilliant and devout monk beloved by the most powerful man in the empire.

She is a foolish child who has just noticed her piglets have grown large and tusked.

She abandons her policy of not accepting invitations from anyone but Leo himself. As Randulf would she embraces the customs of her hosts, eats goose and lamb and even pork, drinks wine (but always less than the others at table). She takes on the manner of an enthusiastic gossip while saying nothing, hearing all. Where before men would wonder what this Brother John was up to, now they say, *He is my friend and his time is spent around my table, by my fire, with my bastard children on his knee.*

As the English Priest would, she takes what she hears and sprinkles it about like holy water. She changes people's minds while they believe they have changed hers, and when a man's case is right she takes it to the Holy Father and pleads on the man's behalf. Where once men said, *He is Leo's pet*, they now say, *It is good to have a friend so close to the Holy Father's ear.*

As Agnes of Mainz would, she longs for the quiet paradise of a monastery library, prays that God will lead her out of this place, let her live the rest of her days as a drop in a vast ocean, another anonymous monk, chanting the offices and copying psalters.

But oh, this tiresome body! Once reacquainted with wine and meat it howls in protest when given broth and water, growls and spasms and refuses to let her rest unless fed and fed and fed.

Oh, tiresome, greedy, needful body! She dines, one evening, with a Roman noble so corrupt, avaricious, immodest and cruel it is all she can do not to overturn his table and set his tapestries ablaze, and yet when this man bids her farewell by holding her shoulders and kissing her cheeks tears flood her eyes and she must turn quickly before he sees how she is affected.

It is a human thing, is it not, she asks God as she walks through the night-calm streets, to crave the touch of another? Jesus hugged the little children, kissed his friends, laid his hands on lepers and invalids. Was it the God in him or the man that used his flesh to comfort and be comforted so?

Never mind the answer. She can no more greet her fellow notaries with a warm embrace than she can climb onto the Pope's lap and ask him to cradle her awhile.

Michaelmas, and the day is filled with processionals and masses spanning the length and breadth of Rome. When at last the obligations are complete and she is in her room about to dress for bed, a messenger arrives summoning her to Leo's apartments. Her eyes itch and her head aches but he is the Holy Father and so what else can she do?

She is admitted to his office, where Leo sits alone on a low couch, without his outer robe and hat, his slippered feet flat on the floor.

'Come, come, sit with me here, Brother John,' he says, and for a terrible moment as she moves to the chair he indicates she is looking down at the white hair wisping over his bald pate. He is an old man and terribly small. Old and small and left alone with a treacherous imposter. Who is looking out for him, this helpless innocent alone and tiny in a palace of fat and canny vipers?

Seated across from him it is better. They are the same height and his eyes front on are clearer and sharper than when she is seated below as usual. Still, his skin, now she is very close, is like the pith on the wild oranges of Aventine Hill. A scrape of her nail would tear it open.

'I have come to notice something curious about you, John.'

'Your Holiness?'

Perhaps his guards are behind the gold-brocade curtains. Perhaps they listen on the other side of the hidden door. She could outrun them, perhaps, but there are others at the end of the corridor, inside the palace entrance, and more outside. She could run but to where and for how long? For what?

'You often beg my favour. More than any other man in my office, I would say. Yet it is always on behalf of others, never yourself.'

Her blood pulses, ready to take flight. She wills it to slow, says, 'Holy Father, I live and work in your presence, in service to Christ our Lord. What is it I would ask for?'

He inhales deeply, gazes hard and fierce into her face. 'With your intercession I have appointed four new abbots and two prelates, moved three bishops to more preferable sees and approved the translation of significant relics from Ravenna and Monte Cassino to the Borgo. I have dissolved an oblate's vows and several prison sentences, granted building contracts and apprenticeships and funded an orphanage and two grammar schools. All this, I have done at your urging.'

'Your wisdom is—'

He raises a hand, continues. 'My agents have made enquiries. We have considered all this at length. Searched for connections and hidden beneficiaries.'

'Holy Father, I—'

'We have found none. It appears you advocate and arrange without personal reward.'

'My reward is in serving the church, serving Your Holiness. Serving Christ. What else could I need?'

'What you need, my dearest child, is to understand that your presence here creates gossip of a most unsavoury kind. A mere Benedictine monk at the right hand of the Pope? It is suspicious, you see.' He smiles and it is the first she has seen from him. It is better that he doesn't. His teeth are jagged and wine-stained, his gums those of a corpse. 'No, you don't see, which is why I must see for you. Foresee, for you!'

Her blood quickens but this time in joy. She is to be dismissed. Sent back to her beloved schola. *Praise to you, my Lord, for answering your humble servant's prayers and allowing me to—*

'Tomorrow you cease to be Brother John. You will become Cardinal Johannes Anglicus, inarguably worthy of a place in the inner sanctum of the Bishop of Rome.'

Ah, my daughter, she imagines God saying—laughing! *You may be the greatest trickster in Rome but you have nothing on me.*

HINGE

THE DAILY WORK of Cardinal Johannes Anglicus is not so different from that of Brother John. She works alongside Leo most hours of most days, leaving his apartment only to deliver messages or take meetings on his behalf. Together they pray the offices and take their meals. Only when it comes time for sleep does she return to her own chamber.

That, too, remains unchanged, though it was necessary to insist. As a cardinal she has been awarded a house in the Borgo, complete with staff, a rose garden, an orchard. It is a gift that cannot be refused and so she accepts gracefully and immediately assigns it to the Schola Francia to be used as a boarding house for visiting clerics and scholars from her homeland. The costs of running the establishment are easily covered by the profits of the vineyard that is also part of her grant. The chateau in Avignon and the estate in Ravenna she leases to minor nobles, uses the income to make endowments to eighteen churches across Rome. That one of these is the church of St Agnes is not a thing a person would think to notice.

What people do notice is her, moving through the Lateran Palace and all of Rome in her sweeping, swishing cardinal's cape. Hard to be humble when your costume draws the admiring eyes of nobles and peasants alike. The scarlet is supposed to signify a willingness to die for the faith but it is far too bold to hold such sombre meaning. It is the red of wet lips, flushed cheeks. Of pinched nipples and swollen labia. In the mirrored walls of the Pope's chamber she sees how the colour makes her straw-coloured hair appear old-man white, her face blank and blanched like a just-washed corpse.

It is her finest disguise yet. Nobody looking upon her could know she is a woman in her prime. Thirty-eight years old, and if she had lived the life her father planned for her she might be a grandmother by now, body bent and worn by childbearing, mind slowed and thickened by decades without intellectual nourishment. What a joy to be here, now, herself. Four years of Roman living have restored the strength lost to her in Athens; her limbs are as sturdy as when she climbed great oaks as a child. Prayer, too, is as easy and thrilling as it was in that long ago forest, and though she sleeps little she always wakes vitalised and ready for the work of interpreting Scripture and weaving its wisdom into sermons and missals, using it to bolster church laws and Christian spirits alike. It is—God knew, He always knows!—exactly what she was made for.

Let the people of Rome see a pale and pampered man of the palace in his showy scarlet cape. Looking back at them from within she is Prisca as the lion lays down at her feet, Thecla as she walks out of the flames and into the desert to preach for seventy years. She is Artemisia sailing into battle with both Persian and Greek flags at the ready.

The cape is only for certain occasions and when she is representing Leo at meetings around Rome. Still, even in her black cassock (softer and better fitted than her old robes), the scarlet piping and sash and the gold ring placed on her finger by the Holy Father himself remind all who cross her path that she is one of the chosen. A hinge upon which the doors of the church swing open. Or shut.

The ambitious, wealthy and powerful who clamour for an audience with the Pope's newest cardinal are easy enough to handle. It's the sincere and wide-eyed young clerics and notaries who fight to serve her in whatever way they can that threaten her composure. Sweet, adoring men from every corner of the known world beg for the opportunity to answer her correspondence, to carry her pens and parchment, to serve her food and wine. Anything Cardinal Johannes Anglicus needs they would be honoured to fetch. Anything he desires they would be eternally grateful to provide. Even to be allowed to sit silent and still in the presence of such a great and holy man would be worth more to them than a purse stuffed with gold.

It does not go unnoticed. Nothing does here. Servius—of course, it would be him—passes as three young monks standing outside her office bicker over who will take Cardinal Anglicus his wine. He tells the story over dinner with half the senior clerics in the Lateran. 'Poor John,' he says, raising his glass towards her, 'surrounded by wine, yet dying of thirst.'

Oh, Lord, but it's hard to keep a lion subdued while circling hordes compete to feed it.

Each night, in her modest room, she strips to her undershift, kneels on a straw mat she has had brought in to lay over the lush carpet so that her crosshatched knees will sting as they should. *Lord Jesus Christ, Son of God, have mercy on me, a sinner*, she repeats until the candle dies.

She continues the prayer from between her sheets, in the hope of staving off prideful fantasies (what Leo will say about the sermon she has written him for Palm Sunday; *Lord Jesus Christ, Son of God, have mercy on me, a sinner*; how the handsome and wise director of the Schola Francia will kiss her ring and perhaps her slippers when she next visits; *Lord Jesus Christ, Son of God, have mercy on me, a sinner*; what Brother Antony would do if he saw her in the scarlet cape; *Lord Jesus Christ, Son of God, have mercy on me, a sinner*; the joy with which any one of those young clerics would respond were she to press her lips to the soft and private skin of his nape; *Oh Lord, Oh Christ, have mercy on me, a sinner, oh mercy mercy mercy*).

JOHN VIII

A JULY MORNING in the year 855 and the air in the Lateran is heavy with something more than the day's building heat. Long before she reaches Leo's apartment she knows something terrible has occurred. The whispers and side glances, a thumping, threatening quiet. Entering the apartment she learns the Holy Father has taken ill in the night. The papal physician has been with him many hours now, leaving only once to collect supplies and an assistant. There have been moans and, once, a scream. His chief chamberlain is weeping, his fellows mutter prayers.

'I will see him,' she says, and because she is a cardinal none stop her.

The smell is at once familiar and mysterious. It grows stronger as she approaches the bed, approaches Leo, less a patriarch than a man, less a man than a melting candle. The physician murmurs about bloodletting and sweating and the application of this herbal paste and that salve while his assistant soaks a cloth in a bucket by the foot of the bed.

'Your Holiness,' she says, kneeling.

'He has not spoken these past hours, Eminence,' the physician says. 'I fear we will not hear his voice again in this life.'

She lifts his hand and it is as dry and cold as a dead man's. 'Father,' she says, and when there is no response she stands, waits for the physician to confirm, then returns to the outer chamber.

'Our Holy Father, Leo IV, has been called home,' she says.

Within the hour, Rome is in turmoil.

The death was so sudden, the Holy Father so healthy, that none in his circle has thought yet of succession. They grieve, those who knew him best, for the man they loved and admired and for the chaos that threatens in his absence.

A *novemdiales* is declared to allow the people to mourn. They flock to the Lateran to weep and pray over their beloved father who lies, dressed in the humble Benedictine robes of his youth, on a raised bier in St Peter's basilica. Attendants burn myrrh and waft swatches soaked in fragrant oil over the body, but it is high summer and by the third day the mourners filing past move ever more quickly to escape the stench. On the fourth day the mass is sung, the casket sealed and Leo IV is interned in St Peter's with the holiest of his successors, all of them safe within the walls he built.

The powerbrokers wait for the nine days of mourning to end, though barely. Before dawn on the tenth day, the square outside the palace fills with campaigners. The *Constitutio romana* of 824 had given all Romans, laity and clergy alike, the right to elect the pope. But this is Rome and those craving influence are as likely to be foreigners as not. The wealthy will offer gold, property, the services of whores, whatever it takes to secure a vote in their interest. Those without money must rely on old-fashioned proselytising, inspirational or fear-mongering speech, heartfelt testimonial, threats and not infrequently blows. The July sun shows no mercy; cardinals, bishops, priests, students and envoys from the old families turn pink, then red. Men faint and are roused with buckets of water so they may continue their pointing and prodding, bullying and wheedling with the glistening skin and bedraggled hair of the drowned.

—

The obvious choice, she believes, is Benedictus. A respectable old cardinal-priest, supported by the noble families, and though not particularly loved by Leo neither was he at odds with him. Besides, the other name most commonly shouted is the traitorous Anastasius. That he has the backing of both emperor and king is undeniable. That he was excommunicated by the recently departed Holy Father and anathematised by two separate synods seems inconsequential to those hungry for Frankish wealth and power.

She imagines a great fresco: in the centre is Leo, his face beatific, as is fitting. Across his shoulders sits a broad beam: on one end balance the Roman nobility, piled on top of each other, arms and legs entangled, mouths open as they constantly voice new iterations of their ancient feuds and entitlements; on the other end is Lothar and his son Louis II, behind them an army of Franks, in front of them a pile of gold. Behind Leo is the city of Rome, safe and prosperous; in front, cowering, are the Saracens, the Northmen, the Lombards, the Byzantines.

She would like to commission an army of painters to raise this fresco on every blank wall throughout Rome. She would like the people to know what it is they risk by choosing badly.

She cannot commission frescoes. She cannot publicly join the debate at all without becoming an easy target for the arrows

Anastasius's men will launch. Cardinal Johannes Anglicus was Pope Leo's pet, they will say. His Valentine. A lowly barbarian monk raised artificially to cardinal by his swooning lover.

What she could do is leave. It is not impossible. She has done it before. The darkest hour of morning, a cloak, a satchel, enough coin to pay her way.

While the campaigning continues in the square, she works with the papal almoner on donations in Leo's name to the poorhouses and orphanages of the city, additional funds and supplies to the student and pilgrim hostels. She insists on a lavishness unseen in Leo's lifetime, unheard of in the history of the alms office. Let Pope Leo IV be remembered as the man of enormous compassion and generosity we all know he was, she tells the almoner and the clerics frowning over their accounts. What can they say? To be mean with this would be to insult the memory of the late and blessed Holy Father.

She checks lists and ledgers and maps, secures packages, joins the nuns as they hand small alms to the beggars on the surrounding streets. She hears the weeping and the prayers for Leo, the sobs of thanks for pitifully small chunks of bread and cheese. On the second day a tiny Italian nun who has worked dawn to dusk without food or water raises a prayer of gratitude for the humble and tireless Cardinal Johannes Anglicus, and a whole crowd of actually humble and tireless women of God line up to kiss her feet.

After that she remains in the alms office bent over the ledgers, mouthing prayers to ward off conversation.

None of this stops her thinking constantly of fleeing. She thinks on it the way she once thought about Antony: imagining over and over the movements, the risks, the rush of life.

She is in her room when Cardinal Servius seeks her out. It is barely daybreak.

'My great regret,' he says, 'is that I was not in Rome during the Holy Father's final day.'

'I am certain he knew well of your love for him,' she says.

'You misunderstand me. My regret is not so small as that. I am not concerned with feelings but with murder.'

She wants to laugh, to spit, to sleep. She settles her breath and her face. 'There was no murder, Eminence, I assure you. Our Lord deemed it time to bring His beloved servant to His side. We who are left behind grieve, but it would be a terrible mistake to let our grief become twisted in this way.'

Servius sneers. 'How convenient it is that only you, *Cardinal*, were with him at the time of his death.'

'Physicians had been attending him throughout the night. And you will know it is not unusual for me to be the earliest at my work and the last to leave.'

'Physicians! Might as well be astronomers or necromancers. They will say mud is water if you throw them a silver coin.

But you!' He jabs the air in front of her face. 'You connived your way into that scarlet cape and then waited for your moment. Waited until those who loved him best were far away. You waited and you struck and now you wait again, a bear in his winter cave, while your disciples do your dirty work below.'

Oh, she is tired. She must sleep. She must leave.

She must leave.

'Ah! He pretends innocence! Of course. Always the innocent, innocent smooth-cheeked Frank! It is the chant of your little soldiers in the square too. Johannes Anglicus—No! *Angelicus* the fools are calling you now—is the only man pure enough for the position. The only one unencumbered by ties and without ambition for himself. Our dear Cardinal Anglicus, who sleeps in a simple cell and gives his riches to the poor and the scholarly!'

Servius may poke his finger right through her eye. He may grasp her throat and lift her by it, shake her body until it shatters, toss the remains out of the window and onto the sunbaked stones below. She finds she does not care. Let him do it. It will be no worse than what he claims her friends are doing to her. A far better end than she will have if they succeed.

She seeks out Benedictus to pledge support, is refused entry to his apartments. His Eminence spends these troubling days in silent prayer. He will not be disturbed until the new Holy Father has been named.

She gathers those notaries and junior clergy who serve her office with such devotion. To a man they tell her she has their vote. 'I beg you to reconsider,' she says, and they tell her they will pray on it. After all, one says, it is God who decides, not men. So we will pray and we will listen. It is telling, though, says another, that you speak with us so directly while Benedictus hides in his room, sends his noble pups to campaign for him. That you give alms and comfort the afflicted while *he* thinks only of himself and his ambitions. It is telling, too, that you have not mentioned that our blessed Leo used his very last breath to pass his crown to you. Save your protests, Eminence. We know this truth for it is spoken all over Rome. We know you are his choice and your humility only affirms his wisdom.

But we will pray on it, Your Eminence. Of course we will.

Prudentius comes. He has aged ten years these last days. He sits heavily, speaks as though it hurts to move his mouth. He tells her she must be ready for a fight.

'I do not want one, Your Eminence. Understand, please, that this is not my will and I do not believe it God's will either. I am not called.'

'I cannot speak for God's will. I can only tell you that the people call for Johannes Anglicus.'

'The people but not the old families. Not the Franks.'

'The old families see that Benedictus has no support in Rome. He is soft as lead and unloved besides. They speak for him because he is one of them. In the end they will cast their votes for you.'

'I will beg them not to.'

Prudentius closes his eyes. 'Anastasius has departed Aachen. The King's men ride with him.'

'Then it is done. He will be elected.'

'I will die to stop him and I will not be alone in it.'

'If it is the will of—'

'It is the will of no one except him and his vile family!'

'And the King.'

'The King does not decide who sits on the throne of St Peter. God decides!'

'Indeed, and in the past He has often agreed with the King.'

'Anastasius will rule for his own interests. You, Johannes Anglicus, will rule for God's people.'

'I will refuse.'

'Then you will doom us all.'

The senior clergy convene in the Lateran basilica as outside in the square the speakers for each faction make their final pleas. It is Prudentius himself who speaks for Cardinal Johannes Anglicus. Inside she cowers against the wall furthest from the crowd. She does not wish to hear the speeches. They have nothing to do with her. Cannot.

There is a relative hush and then a roar. A hush, a larger roar. Hush, roar. This is the sound of the final *acclamatio*, overseen by the three men responsible for all Lateran business when the throne is vacant—the archpriest, archdeacon, and *primicerius* of the notaries. Hush, roar. Hush, roar. There are more candidates than she realised, or else the roars are inconclusive and operatives are scurrying through the crowd to prod volume or force silence before the next round.

She examines the floor beneath her feet. Porphyry—imperial purple, papal purple—taken from the Pantheon four hundred years ago, from Egypt a millennium earlier. The ground beneath my feet is older than humanity's saving, she thinks. It has outlived every man who has stood upon it.

Crystals deep in the stone spark like the sun has hit them. She looks towards the apse to determine how the rays have penetrated so far into the packed church. The eyes of all are on her and she sees at once how it must appear. This slight hooded figure, modestly and meekly looking down, and only when the light of heaven illuminates him does he look up and out at the awestruck assembly.

The cries go out. Cries and crying. Wails and weeping. Her name. The latest of her names, filling the space as surely and miraculously as the light had a moment before.

None of this is real. She touches her stomach where the boar ran through. Perhaps she never left the fog that came over her then. Perhaps she is dreaming all this even now.

'Your Eminence, you must speak,' says someone at her elbow while others push her forward.

She shakes off the hands that would raise her up. She turns from the path cleared for her and runs.

She doesn't know she is heading for St Agnes's church, all the way across the city and outside of the walls, until she is mere strides away on Via Nomentana. She collapses in front of her namesake's altar, presses her forehead to the stone over the child saint's tomb, prays that God will remove the devil's veil from the eyes of all those in the Lateran. Lord, forgive them their blasphemy and guide them to Your proper Prince. Lord, please, let this cup pass from me.

She is still there hours later when they come for her.

They say the light remains brightly over the place she kneels though the sun has long set.

They say it is just like humble John to seek guidance here of all places. On the golden apse above, a nimbed St Agnes shimmers, a halo-less pope attends her on each side. These most powerful men, less important to Christ than a child who loves Him more than her life. What wisdom Cardinal Anglicus has to pray on this lesson in humility before taking the highest of thrones.

They lift her above their heads to carry her back to the Lateran.

Now is when this ends, she thinks, holy hands on my calves and behind my knees. I should have kept running past the church, through the outer suburbs, shedding my robes as I went. Given a trader my rings to let me hide under his cartloads. Bounced out of the carriage when the trader would not notice and found a cave near a stream. Sustained myself on water and river weeds while my hair grew long. Stolen a horse and ridden like the Huns, not dismounting even to eat but warming raw meat under the saddle as I went.

Instead this. Palms curved around her buttocks and flattened beneath her lower back. Fingers clutching her arms, grazing the side of breasts she has not acknowledged in years. *Now* this ends *now* they will know me *now* and it is *now* the moment of my unmasking and very soon must be the moment of my death.

A new day is breaking as they carry her through Rome while people cheer and weep and shout her false name. They are truly blessed, the people tell each other, to have God so clearly indicate His vicar. Rome, all Christendom in fact, is blessed that the chosen one is a truly pious and humble servant of the servants of God.

Although there is great risk in crowning a new pope without the emperor's approval, the cardinals determine that the risk of Anastasius and his supporters arriving in Rome and demanding a new election is greater. The coronation must happen at once.

Someone washes her feet. Directs her behind a golden screen to change into new undergarments, a new shift and startling white cassock. When she emerges someone drapes on her a robe the rich shining purple of lamb's blood with gold thread woven through, the silk so soft if she closes her eyes she can't be sure it covers her.

She is led to a mule caparisoned with gold and purple. The saddle that holds her could feed the thousands lining the streets for months. Dirty and dripping with sweat, faces and arms burnt by the terrible sun in which they've waited to catch sight of their pope. They should mob the procession and throw her to the ground. Sell the saddle to feed their babies, tear the jewels from her hands and throat, buy wood enough for seven winters.

In front of St Peter's the mule is halted and hands of infinite gentleness help her dismount. Men in red and black line the sacred stairway on their knees. She must let them kiss the hem of her robe. She must resist the urge to kick their puckered lips.

At the narthex she is told to kneel. A crown is placed on her head. There is no removing the title that comes with it until the day she dies.

Inside the basilica smells of pine and wood smoke and she is in the forest of Mainz, piglets running merry across her lap. Hands close over each elbow and urge her forward and she has never been further from that girl in the woods.

'A significant moment,' says Prudentius, who is the cause of all this. 'Never before has an Englishman entered this church as pope.'

'And neither will one today,' she murmurs.

'Of English born,' he says as they move past hundreds of silent observers.

Behind the throne stands Randulf, shaking with silent laughter. She looks away and back and he is gone. She sits on the throne, looks at nothing in particular, the church and the people in total. Her church. Her people. Is she supposed to speak? It is unthinkable.

Prudentius steps forward and speaks and time speeds up. She is led from the throne to a rough wooden stool on which she must lower herself as if shitting, a reminder that even the Pope is subject to the laws of nature. Her knees and hips ache with the pose while priests move about waving burning straw to symbolise the impermanence of all worldly states and beings.

She cannot see how she might ever leave this place alive.

The papal apartment. Hers, forever. The outer rooms more familiar to her than any others in Rome; the bedchamber she has only entered once, the day of Leo's death. Then she had eyes only for him, had not noticed the utter decadence of the space in which he lay. The bed, blanketed in lush, glimmering furs, could sleep a whole family with ease. When she sits on it her feet dangle far from the ground and she feels for a moment like a child. Then she notices the mirrors hanging high around the bed and is a grown woman once more. A woman who knows, as a pope or monk should not, what use such a bed could be put to, the frescoes that could be created, reproduced in triplicate on those perfectly positioned mirrors.

Scattered about the room are small tables of marble, stone and wood, some displaying bejewelled cups and crystal vases, others laden with fruit, meat, wine and bread. As though one might become starved during the night. From the effort of sleeping? Ha!

And here by the bed, draped across a chair encrusted with precious stones she cannot name, is a robe of pure white silk. It is impossible not to imagine it sliding across bare skin. Impossible in this space not to remember all the fleshly pleasures she has spent most of her adult life trying to forget.

Oh, how Randulf would love this room. This moment. She wills him to appear as he did in the church but he will not. She can call the chamberlain and be brought anything she wishes, but she cannot see Randulf again. She cannot know what it is to reach this place and have a friend alongside to see it with her.

UNHEARD OF AUDACITY

(855-857)

RESURRECTION

WITH THE EXCEPTION of Prudentius, who becomes chief adviser to the Bishop of Rome, those who fought for her to be here are no longer part of her life; it is not done to have mere students, monks and notaries in the highest realm on earth. Her old sparring partners now speak of her as infallible. She has secretaries and courtiers and servants. Deacons and bishops are her willing slaves. Leo had spoken once of the loneliness of power, but he had her, and she has no one. Nor can she, for any man who knows her true self enough to be called friend would, in knowing that true self, become her enemy. She is the most powerful person in the world. She is barely a person at all.

The days roll on. She reads and sleeps and eats, all of it more often surrounded by men than she would like. She holds meetings in which cardinals beg for larger property grants and bishops beg to become cardinals. She writes letters to Randulf and to her father then burns the parchment in her personal hearth. Parchment to burn, a fire of one's own to burn it in. Such is life for the Vicar of Christ.

She prays, of course. In front of crowds of worshippers and in her private chapel with her closest advisers and every morning and night alone in her bedchamber and silently during meetings and meals and while walking the vast, lonely halls of the Lateran, she prays and prays and prays and prays. She might as well be writing more letters to burn in the hearth. Since the crown was placed on her head, God is gone from her as surely as everyone else she has loved.

Two months into her papacy Anastasius arrives in Rome, spoiling for a fight. Laughing like a child he bounds up the steps of St Peter's, swings his sword at the panels Leo had installed illustrating the excommunication of his former protégé. He barely chips the paint. His retinue is a third of the size it was rumoured to be; no surprise once it becomes known that Emperor Lothar is dying in a monastery and his son, Louis, is entirely occupied with shoring up his power against the claims of his brothers. As for Anastasius's supporters in Rome, they have, for the most part, moved on from the election to the next noble intrigue.

Anastasius's threat to cut the false pope's throat becomes, after a week, a demand for a meeting, which becomes after another week a request to be allowed to return to his priesthood at St Marcellus.

Against the advice of her cardinals she meets with the man who is both a scheming, ambitious little rat and the only man in Rome whose Greek scholarship comes close to her own. It is a waste to send him away, as well as a risk. Best to keep him close, keep him busy.

Rome is astonished by the news that Pope John VIII has named his would-be assassin and usurper the abbot of Santa Maria as well as assigning him the job of translating several weighty Greek philosophies and *vitas* into Latin for the Lateran library. Truly they are blessed with a pope of wisdom, yes, but also mercy. Truly, it is impossible to see how any other man alive could sit so rightly on the throne of St Peter.

On Sundays and feast days, of which there are exhaustingly many, she conducts the stational liturgy, processing from the Lateran to whichever church has been assigned to that day, that saint. Each time she processes—sometime on mule, sometimes on foot, always surrounded by priests and cardinals, bishops and monks—the people of Rome line the streets calling for blessings, alms, intercession, justice. The people are expensively dressed and well spoken, the babies they raise up for blessing fat and rosy-cheeked. Or they are grey-faced and ragged, their Latin mangled and childish, their babies shrivelled and baggy-eyed. Noble, merchant or beggar, the desperation in their faces does not change. Nor do the things they ask from their pope: illness cured, a hardy child, financial abundance, a lighter heart.

Only the last can she provide. She tells the people to love God and pray often, to give alms if they can and act with kindness always. She tells them God sees their suffering and is with them always. God loves you, she says, and in their faces she sees that they think *she* is *Him*. They weep with gratitude and beg to touch her robe, kiss her feet. They kneel in the filth of the street and say, *The Holy Father gazed upon me Oh I am blessed I am blessed Thank you God.*

Is this why You could not stay with us down here, Lord Jesus? she asks. You thought looking people in the face would bring You closer to humanity, but they are so undiscerning in their adoration, so pitiful in their desperation, that You felt further apart from them than ever.

God does not answer. Not there on the street beside the weeping, devoted masses. Not as she processes into the church behind priests bearing candles and thuribles. Not as she sings with the choir or recites the Canon of the Mass. She knows the congregation is moved; their love surges towards her like a building storm. She offers it to God, begs him to take what is His. All is silence; the deluge of their devotion is hers alone.

In September the sickly Lothar renounces his throne, naming his eldest son, Louis II, emperor in his place. Within days Lothar is dead and it is reported that his last act was, in fact, the division of his empire between his three sons. Did the man learn nothing from his father's mistakes? From Fontenoy and the decade of murder and pillage that followed?

She is repulsed by the whole squabbling, grasping lot of them, privately curses every Carolingian ruler from her father's beloved Charles down.

Pope John VIII, of course, sends condolences to the bereaved son, his blessings and joyful tidings to the new ruler of them all. Invites Louis to Rome for a coronation in the tradition of his adored and revered great-grandfather Charles. Plans a celebration such that he will be flattered into forgetting the anointing is supposed to go the other way, that this pope was elected without regnal approval or confirmation.

The day after Michaelmas in the year 856. Another Friday, another endless round of appointments at which she must sit and listen to pointless men offer meaningless tributes in order to extract invented titles. She no longer bothers to look ahead at the day's agenda; there is nothing she need ever prepare. Either she knows the man and what he deserves—or not—at once, or she says she must make enquiries. Always she says she must pray before answering. She considers posting a sign in the outer chamber reminding all that only the Lord can provide so they should go and pray on their promotions and gold-hunger themselves. But, then, if the supplicants stop she will have even less to distract her from the utter silence in her heart.

She no longer bothers to look ahead at the agenda and so it is not until the man who has just kissed her slipper stands and she sees his face clearly that she knows Randulf of Fulda is alive and in Rome.

'Your Holiness,' he says.

She tells the chamberlain to clear the room. There is a pause, then a flurry of movement. She studies his face: older and tireder but unmistakably him, not a ghost or a revenant or the laughing spectre of her coronation imagining.

'It is true then,' he says when they are alone. 'My wild little trickster Agnes on the throne of St Peter.'

Her name. His voice. That gaze holding hers without hesitation. She is forty years old and the Bishop of Rome; she is an unmarriageable sixteen-year-old girl from Mainz with dreams of sainthood.

'Brother Randulf,' she says: calm, authoritative, papal. 'I thought you dead.'

'I almost was. Bandits on the road. I was senseless for months, cared for by the wife of a village priest. The barely literate cleric sent a message to the abbot that only sowed confusion. The stolen manuscripts were sold for a pittance at Monte Cassino. Conclusions were drawn.'

He speaks so lightly. Each easy sentence contains a story she wants spun out at length. All these stories yet to read in a book she thought long finished.

'I thank God that you live, brother,' she says. 'It is a true blessing to see you.'

He laughs. More a scoff. 'Get down from there.' He reaches up and grabs her hand, tugs on it so that she must climb down from her throne or fall.

'I could have you cast in the dungeons for that,' she says, standing eye to eye with him. Their hands remain clasped. He must surely feel the tremor in her.

'I could have *you* tried for treason and blasphemy and a whole lot more besides.'

'So we each have the means to destroy each other.'

'It has always been so,' he says.

'And yet here we both are.'

She calls her chamberlain back, tells him to relocate all the staff to Cardinal Prudentius's apartment, to order fresh wine and bread and cheese and fruit. The Holy Father will spend the remains of the day in prayer and conference with his oldest friend.

'The gossips of Rome will be in paroxysms,' she tells Randulf, leading him to her bedchamber. 'Pious John alone with a Frank.'

'I suppose they are used to you being alone with Romans only.'

'I am never alone with anyone except God.'

'Never?'

'No.'

'I am sorry for you,' he says. 'I have been alone hardly at all since you left.'

'Benedictines rarely are.'

'That is not what I meant.'

'I know what you meant.'

She would like to examine every new line on his face, but instead she removes her cap and cloak and places them on their stand. She pours and drinks a cup of mint-laced water, says, 'I thought you dead all these years, Randulf. That you've been alive and fucking the whole time brings me great joy.'

A small laugh. 'You do not speak like a pope.'

'You have known so many, of course.'

'You look like one, though. Old and tired and overfed.'

'Imagine thinking I might care you find me unlovely when all I care about is that you live and that I have been allowed to know this.'

His eyes have not stopped roaming the room since he entered. Now, at last, he turns to her. 'I did not say I find you unlovely, only much changed. When I heard John the Englishman of Fulda, lately of Athens, was the new head man I pictured this skinny, husky-voiced girl stomping around in the papal tiara and it seemed too absurd to be true. I forgot you have lived a whole life since I saw you, become as aged and sexless as any other Hermetic.' He lifts his hands, presses one to each of her cheeks. 'Utterly convincing.'

'My guards are right outside,' she says, folding her hands over his, drawing them away from her face. 'If I scream you will be dead before you can draw another breath.'

Randulf kisses her forehead, her eyelids, her lips. 'I trust you will take care, then, to be quiet.'

She *is* old and tired and overfed, and God knows she has striven harder than most to be sexless. Had succeeded, she thought. Look where she is! Who she is! None of it possible if she had not conquered the flesh, starved the hungry kitchen dog into submission.

And yet. His lips press against her skin and she is neither old nor young but only Agnes, who is loved and known by Randulf. He removes her cassock and shift, unbinds her breasts and kisses that long-shunned flesh and she is not dog nor pope but simply, softly human. He undresses with clumsy, shameless urgency, and when he presses against her his heart pounds hard like the miracle it is. She opens to him, draws his resurrected body into her abandoned one.

Oh, Lord, I ask you, what is this if not a sacrament?

'Have you truly not laid with another in all these years?' he asks when she is dressed once more and has retrieved food and wine from the outer room.

'Truly.'

'Of the many astonishing facts of your life I find this hardest to accept.'

She places the platter and jug on a marble chest. 'Many of our brothers and sisters in God go their whole lives, Randulf. It is not so unusual.'

'Sheep do as shepherds tell them. Wolves make their own path and it is more often than not one scattered with bodies.'

'As yours is?'

'I am a hunting hound at best. You could rip my throat out without slowing your pace. Did so, more or less.'

She hands him a goblet of wine. 'I see you remain prone to dramatics.'

'So says the woman who starts and ends her days with men bowing to kiss her silk-clad feet. And you cannot deny the brutality. To leave a man in love without a backward glance.'

'It was the love I left, not the man.'

'The man was crushed all the same.'

'I am sorry for him, truly.' She kisses him, touches his beloved face.

He moves away, says, 'It is some consolation to know you've never loved another. That I ruined you as much as you me.'

'Randulf, please. All this talk of crushing and ruin, throats ripped out and scattered bodies! My leaving you was the saving of us both. You continue to live more freely and well than any Benedictine should and I, well, I am married to Christ, father to all of His children.'

'I will concede,' he says, reaching past her to take a grape from the platter, 'that your present circumstances are somewhat a vindication.'

'Somewhat, yes. And now—oh, Randulf!—it is a blessing beyond blessings that we have found each other again.'

It *is* a blessing. Though God remains silent, this is proof He is watching over her still. He saw His pope losing her heart for this world, sent the only person who could know what it once was and so restore her to herself.

'Blessing beyond blessings,' Randulf echoes, places his hands on her waist, his mouth to her throat. Her body responds to his touch like a starved crowd to the sound of the dispensator's cart. He smiles at her greed, holds her grasping hands at her sides. He blows cool air onto her lips, laughs as she strains towards him.

'What would you do,' he says, 'if I were to lay you down right here on this carpet then shout for the guards the moment

I entered you? Would you throw me off and cover yourself? Accuse me of sodomitic outrage?' He kisses her, presses his hardness against her stomach. 'Or would you tell them to wait by the door while I rut the need out of you?'

'Try it and see,' she says, bites him hard on the mouth.

He presses her down, sinks inside her fast and deep.

'You would do it, wouldn't you? Tell the guards to call the cardinals and prepare the dungeon just so long as they let you finish. You would be martyred for this.'

She moans her assent. Means it or doesn't. She is insensible, which is his point, is it not? She can't think and doesn't wish to. If he stops moving she may indeed rip out his throat.

There is no danger of that. He is again all grunt and breath. A boy on the riverbank thrusting an earthquake into existence. A young adventurer kissing her scars while his fingers show her the wonder of flesh. A weeping would-be husband clinging to her near-drowned body in a filthy island church. He is all of them and she is nothing and everything at once, an animal thrashing in the mud without knowing why, a creature of God soaring past the angels themselves.

'Agnes,' he cries into her. 'Agnes, my only. My true and only wife.'

He is who he always was. Sentimental and arrogant. And, always, always her greatest friend.

'It is right what you said earlier,' she says. 'You did ruin me. Made it so I could never be happy with another.'

He smiles, smug, sated, sleepy. She kisses his forehead. She will let him rest there on her carpet a few minutes more, then she really must send him on his way. Already the palace, if not all of Rome, will be in fits about the mysterious visitor. She kisses his forehead again and prays for God to protect and save him. Kisses him again and again as he snores, and she is glad she said what she did about his ruining her, even though it is not true, or not in the way he understands.

He knows her better than anyone has and ever will but even he can never grasp that he ruined her long before he pushed her down in the reeds. Ruined her and was the making of her at once on the first night she met him. There at her father's table he asked her about iconoclasts and she knew what it was for a man to treat her as a person and in doing so made it impossible she could ever tolerate anything else again.

HUMMINGBIRD

RANDULF STAYS EIGHT days in Rome, sleeping in the Schola Francia boarding house, meeting scholars and scribes all over the Borgo and, as everyone from her council of advisers to the laundresses would tell you, spending all the hours between Compline and Nocturnes in the Holy Father's private chamber.

Nobody asks her the nature of these private meetings. Do they not dare or is there is no need? Everyone knows the look of the sex-drunk. Everyone knows you're as likely to see it in the Lateran as not.

She feels no sorrow at Randulf's leaving. He will return in the summer and until then he will write to her. He will write to His Holiness John VIII, that is, and his letters will be dry and impersonal so as not to excite the half-dozen assistants who will read them before her. Nevertheless, every time she receives one of his letters she will know that he still lives, and that he knows who she is, and this will be enough.

She feels no sorrow at his leaving; her staff make no secret of their great relief. They have been gathering reports that bad omens abound. A plague of locusts in the French countryside. Three days and nights of blood rain in Brescia. Earthquakes in Metz, Paderborn and Arles. September snow in Ravenna. And in the Leonine City, she is told, this whole last week owls have hooted from the rooftops all night long.

'Enough!' she tells the doomsayers. 'You are so intent on finding omens you neglect the suffering of the people.' She issues instructions, signs orders, releases funds: grain to replace that devoured by locusts; a delegation to investigate the claims of blood rain and to comfort the frightened; food and building materials to the quake-struck; grain, again, to replace snow-covered crops in Ravenna. As for the owls, the Greeks would say they are a good omen, in fact. Protectors of the city.

'The pagan Greeks might say so,' a notary mutters. After an airless pause adds, 'Your Holiness.'

'How amusing. An infant Roman claims to know more about Greek religion than a man who spent eight years in holy community there and who also, I should not need to remind you, is the Vicar of Rome and head of the Christian world by Divine Right.'

She has never spoken so harshly to her staff and it shows on their faces. The boy who spoke is shaking and his fellows appear ready to kick him to death. She lets the silence hang until the room feels on the point of self-combustion.

'It is unconscionable,' she says, 'that my very own people waste time like this while Christians suffer. Move! At once! There is much work to be done. And you'—she need not point or name him, the insolent, quivering child—'will be personally responsible for the recovery in Paderborn. I expect you to oversee the operation at every step, to personally ensure aid goes to those most in need and to report back to me, in detail, about the situation there.'

She watches with a deep, unfamiliar pleasure as the waves pass over his disloyal face: relief, pride, then horror as he understands his exile. It is a sin, of course, to enjoy the suffering of others. She will pray on it later.

For all the good it'll do.

None of her staff raise bad omens again. If they did she could outdo them, for there are mischief demons running amok in her very body. A month after Randulf's departure her stomach begins to violently expel all but bread and water. A month on from that the kitchen staff suspect the Holy Father has an entire family secreted in his chamber, so enormous are the quantities of goose pie and spiced cream he orders. This while he is still eating his fill and then some at meals shared with his council and clerics. Meanwhile, every bit of the extra food appears to be settling on her breasts. They push against their bindings, and when she adds an extra strip of linen the pressure makes her whimper with the pain of it.

Forty days after Epiphany. The double feast of the Purification of the Blessed Virgin Mary and the Presentation in the Temple. A reminder that even the mother of Christ required purification after the filth of birth; even Jesus needed to be introduced to the church.

Day has not yet broken and her hands sting with cold as she lights the candles of her cardinals in the sacristy of St Martina. They walk in silence to St Hadrian the Martyr, where lower clergy and laity from every church in Rome await them. All the ancient monuments of Rome and all the gold and jewels of the Lateran combined cannot come close to the beauty and wonder of this mass of men, stone-still in the cold dark while the flames in their hands spark and spar.

She pauses to take it all in before the full procession must start, and in this moment of grateful stillness a hummingbird takes flight deep within her. She holds her breath, waits for the sensation to return.

The clear, cool voice of the schola leader breaks the silence with *Exsurge Domine*.

Arise O Lord, the faithful sing as she and her men enter the church. *As it was in the beginning, is now, and ever shall be, world without end.*

The deacon chants the *Flectamus Genua* as she reaches the altar, and there it is again. Yes. The tiny flutter of tiny wings.

When her duties are finished and she is alone in her room (chamberlains and guards outside the door; cardinals and notaries buzzing throughout the apartment) she rests hands on her bare flesh. Waits. There! Oh, Lord, it is unmistakable.

She cannot recall the last time she bled. For a time its monthly coming was a gauge of God's approval. With each batch of barely bloodied leaves she dropped into the Fulda latrine pit she prayed He would continue to bless her deception, until, at some unremembered point, she began to take the ease of concealment for granted. By the time she arrived in Athens, she did not think of it at all, the shedding of a little blood no more meaningful than other evacuations of bodily waste.

Such a small inconvenience, really, that she barely noticed its slowing during her hungry years, its failure to appear at all some months since she's been in Rome. How could it matter one way or the other?

Yet here it is: the hummingbird flutter.

Sarah, Rebecca, Rachel, she thinks. All older than she is now.

Sarah, Rebecca, Rachel. All barren until God decided they were not.

She hears her prankster God laughing harder than ever. Despite everything, she feels joy that His silence has ended.

REMEDIES

THERE ARE REMEDIES. The market wives of Mainz would know. Alerted by a tilt of the head towards the belly, a veiled remark about stopped blood, any one of them would whisper the name of the wise woman who might help, or offer the recipe for a brew to restore her to rights.

She has read such recipes in medical texts over the years. All recorded, likely, by men not as expert as they believed. She remembers, vaguely, a potion of parsley, hartwort, rue and celery seeds. Lovage and thyme in there as well, perhaps. Artemisia has a reputation; it's said you will always find a supplier within hark of a whorehouse. But how it is to be ingested or applied she does not know.

RAPTURE

What good is knowing, anyway? The Pope cannot simply walk to the market and buy such provisions, nor request them from the cooks lest they are wise to the purpose. Certainly she cannot ask the physicians. She is all powerful yet helpless as a newborn lamb.

There are surely many in this palace of men who have put women in this condition and expected the evidence to be removed, but that is no help. Even if she could confide (and she cannot, of course, she cannot), not one among them would have lifted a finger to make the removal happen nor given a single moment's thought to how it might be so. She has become, in thought and friendship and knowledge, one of these men. Knowing such things are done by women, but with no clue as to how.

She sends a message to Randulf urging his immediate return for reasons that will be explained in person. The request itself as well as the order to use the relay network reserved for missives to kings and archbishops causes a palace full of raised eyebrows and whispers. There is nothing to be done about that. Without his assistance, and soon, there is little hope.

For nine days it rains and the Tiber swells and swells. The Romans on her staff insist the river can take weeks more of this. On the tenth day the banks burst. Boats, bridges and half the houses of Campus Martius are drowned on impact. By the twelfth day the water has reached the doors of Santa Maria in Via Lata—the very place blessed St Paul was held during his persecution—and there is great fear that the ancient stone of the crypts may not hold. Already lesser structures have been inundated, and corpses of every vintage float through the streets.

I have lived this before, she thinks. The rain doesn't stop, the streets become part of the river, the saved and damned alike are exhumed. The hungry gather outside the gates in hope while the good Christians inside pray for relief instead of providing it. Water bogs every home and hall, turns every ordinary scratch into a murderous pestilence.

There is a saint who laid hands on a repentant pregnant nun and the child dissolved as if it had never been. *Healed*, the *vita* said. The pregnancy was healed. It is absurd but miracles always are. She cannot remember the name of the saint. Never mind; who needs intercession when you have a direct line to God? What do you say, Lord? Will you heal your pope of this affliction? Dissolve the issue without harm?

A surge of warmth, a rush of love. Her hands go to her belly, feel the flutter, the wonder. Why should you want this gone,

God is saying, when it is the very thing that has brought us back into communion?

The messenger returns with a reply from Fulda. Brother Randulf remains abroad on his work for the abbey, having overwintered in Hibernia. The Holy Father's message will of course be forwarded to him in haste when they receive word of his return to the Continent.

It is the first of March, winter a full month behind them in Rome, but in those far-off northern islands it may linger far longer.

All that night she is tormented by visions of that poor girl birthing to death in Mainz, of her own mother whose dying screams haunted the English Priest until the end of his life.

In the morning light she reminds herself that not all births end in death. Perhaps not even most.

Still, it is hard to believe this one won't.

The locust swarm has moved south, destroying any hope of grain enough to feed Rome let alone export to the suffering northerners. Worse! Witnesses report seeing clouds of insects descend on small children, smother them in an instant, strip the flesh off their bones. In the churches, parents kneel in grief only to have the locusts invade, suck the moisture from their weeping eyes before devouring the holy bread and sacred candles. In northern Italy sturdy roofs cave in under the weight of the fat insatiable creatures.

'Holy Father, we know you do not wish to hear of omens,' Prudentius says, a flock of stern-faced cardinals behind him, 'but we have consulted all the histories and never have there been signs such as these.'

She nods, resists the impulse to touch her belly. Any day now the crucifix around her throat will burst into flames. At any moment, eucharist wine will turn to mud in her mouth.

News from Constantinople that Michael, all of sixteen years old, has deposed his own mother. Theodora has put up no resistance, retiring quietly to a convent. Lucky Theodora, she thinks, to have experienced the heights of glory and still be allowed to end your life reading and drinking watered wine with other happily powerless crones.

Leave leave leave beat the wings in her womb. She scours the *Liber Pontificalis* for precedent.

Beginning with St Peter, for three centuries every pope ended in martyrdom. Since then there has been a single nominal renunciation, six hundred years ago. Nominal because Pontianus was a prisoner of the anti-Christian emperor at the time and beaten to death soon after. Half a century on, Marcellinus was said to have renounced not the throne but God himself while a captive of Diocletian. Happily for his soul, he renounced the renunciation and he, too, was swiftly put to death.

You would be martyred for this, Randulf said.

In the midst of a tedious, hours-long discussion about the repair of flood-damaged churches she is hit with an impulse so powerful it can only be a direction from God.

'I must go on retreat,' she says to her cardinals. 'An extended time of silent prayer and contemplation. Ostia or Monte Cassino, perhaps. Somewhere I will be undisturbed, able to commune more deeply with God. To learn what is meant by these omens. To hear what God is trying to tell us, what He wants us to do.'

There is a long silence during which the hummingbird flutters and pecks with fervour and it is hard to believe that the gathered men cannot sense the new soul among them.

Prudentius is the first to speak, says, 'Holy Father, the power of your prayer is well-known and a profound gift to us all. I fear, alas, that your absence at this difficult time will cause panic among the people. They will consider it a bad omen in itself to have the See vacant.'

'I will explain it to them,' she says. 'A public address in the square to let them know their father is not abandoning them but entering into spiritual battle for their protection.'

'Holy Father, forgive me,' says Nicholas, the oldest amongst her cardinals, a survivor of the terrors of 846. 'Anastasius lurks still. He pretends loyalty but only because you are strong and beloved by the people. If you leave Rome at a time of such unrest he will take his chance, gather allies, stir dissent.'

Let him, she thinks. Let him take the throne, the Lateran, the city. He is clever and charismatic, gifted in languages and better educated than any man in this room. A fine choice for pope, apart from the treason and excommunication.

'Your arguments are sound,' she tells the men. 'I am bound to follow God, however, and His will is clear. He would have me retreat, to pray and meditate at length as I did in Athens. And so I must.'

Prudentius allows himself a sigh and she allows it to pass without comment.

'What He wills, will be, Holy Father,' says Prudentius. 'I will instruct the *vicedominus* to begin preparations, send envoys to ascertain which of our houses in the country has sufficient staff to assure your comfort. The *primicerius* will need to know, of course. The archpriest.'

'The *superista*,' Nicholas adds. 'I will meet with him at once. We will need extra guards in the palace once it is known the throne is vacant. As well as a retinue of the best men to accompany you, Holy Father, of course.'

She almost laughs. Had she thought they would let her pack a satchel and walk into the wilderness alone? That she would be left unobserved long enough to birth her child? And then what? She would wander back to the Lateran with some newborn foundling in her arms?

No. She had not thought that, not really. She had only thought—felt—*retreat retreat retreat* and the urgency of it had let her think it was of God. She sees now that it is impossible and therefore cannot be divine. As Prudentius said, *What He wills, will be.*

Before anyone can begin preparations she announces the plan is cancelled. Consternation over this uncharacteristic indecisiveness is outweighed by relief that the Holy Father will remain in his rightful place.

Mid-April and still no word from Randulf. Her body is a wonder. The boar's marks grow with her, just as in her sprouting youth. The dense, dark scarring stretches into pale rivers across her rounding belly. The change in her shape is not yet evident when she is in cassock, robe and cape but it can only be a matter of weeks.

—

There is no choice to make; God has made it for her, as of course He always does whether she is humble enough to admit it or not. What she must make is a plan. It will not be a safe or sure one, but that, too, is beyond her control.

She studies the liturgical calendar and the *Ordines Romani*. Less than two weeks hence is the Rogation Litany, which calls for a procession extravagant enough to put the pagan emperors to shame. There will be singing and drums to scare off the devil, reliquaries paraded before the crowds, painted icons and statues held aloft. She will dress, beneath her violet ceremonial robes, in her simplest white alb, which is similar enough to that of a priest to fool a layman. When the rituals and ceremonials are complete she will insist on walking unprotected among the people. She will shower the crowd with every drop of her famed charisma, preach with the fervour and passion for which she became known in her earliest days in this city. She will create a frenzy of worship as only she can, put a thousand faithful Romans between her and the Pope's entourage. And in its midst, somehow—God willing, God willing—she will discard her robes, become a simple parish priest. She will do what she should have done on the day of her election. She will run.

A CURIOUS THING

ROGATION DAY AND all of Rome is out awaiting the procession of their pope. This, despite the locust dust that hangs over the city, making the clear morning dusky, finding its way into throats and eyes so every third person is red-eyed and coughing. The haze can only aid her disappearance and she thanks God for it as she is driven to St Peter's, where she climbs the steps and begins the Litany of the Saints before mounting the waiting mule and continuing throughout the city.

Here, on the back of the mule which froths and splutters at the dust but never stops moving steadily, following the procession of white-robed priests carrying the cross and various statues, the cardinals in their scarlet, the abbots and monks, barefoot and dusty, and behind her the nuns and deaconesses, lower clergy, soldiers and, at last, the common people—here, now, she is struck with the knowledge that she does not exist.

It is not like in Athens where, after months of fasting and meditating on the endless plummet to hell, she held the perfect joyous understanding that there was no such thing as the self. This knowledge is new and utterly terrible. She does not exist because if she did she could choose to attend to the searing heat that has announced itself in her body. She could halt the animal beneath her, ask one of the hundreds in her service to help her to the ground, bring her something cold to drink, call, perhaps, a physician to attend.

She cannot do any of these things any more than a serpent's heart can choose to leave its body while that body is still in motion.

The writhing serpent chants in a hundred languages and one of them is Latin, which is what continues to come from her own mouth along with an alarming amount of green bile which must be splattering over her fine rogation cope of pale violet. If she existed she could decide to look, but she is the serpent's heart and she pulses without direction or decision.

Holy Father, are you ill? someone says, and there are hands upon her and cool water on her brow and lips and she is herself again, is the Pope again. She is herself, yes, and herself is in terrible, terrible trouble of a kind that cannot be hidden. This is why the men around her clamour to shield her from the crowd even as they continue to march, urge her mule forward. *Holy Father, we will soon be at the Lateran Your Holiness we are near done with the liturgy Holy Father I will hold your back hold your legs hold you upright Holy Father May Lord God keep you we are not so far from home.*

The procession moves forward and the mule spits locust wings onto the backs of the barefooted Benedictines. She closes her eyes, lets a dozen hands hold her. She thinks of last October, Randulf in her bed. She asked him if he ever thought about that old stone church on the road to Marseille. How they stumbled towards it, early evening, near starved, met with the whimsically arranged bodies of men, women and children killed with force and glee by some passing band of Northmen or savage, savaged men who were lately brave soldiers.

'It is strange,' Randulf had said. 'In the days afterwards I thought I would never again close my eyes without seeing the piles of dead, never eat without tasting the rot on my tongue. It played over and over in my mind until one day I realised that while it still caused me distress it was not more than if the story had been told to me by another.

'This is how we go on, I realised, playing and replaying

events. We wear the horror out of it, make it a curious thing that happened to someone, somewhere, once.'

'Yes,' she agreed, 'that is what it was: a curious thing that happened once.'

'And in heaven it will not even be that. *For there, past troubles will be forgotten and hidden from my eyes.*'

'You dare to quote Scripture to the Apostolic Lord, brother?' she said, and they were light and joyful together, the deep running poison of that terrible church seeping out in their laughter and sighs.

She thinks of this now in the relentless heat that comes from inside with all of Rome pulsing towards her and dust and insect wings in her eyes and nose and throat, and as well, *dear Lord save me*, now it is as though all the locusts in creation have risen from the dead in her womb, a swarm the size of Francia pushing to escape their fleshy tomb as she thinks *what a curious thing a thing that happened to someone somewhere once.* The locusts surge with the force of a boar and she thinks *just another curious thing that happened dear Lord save me to someone not me this is an event in history I will tell to Randulf a curious thing Lord Jesus God save me save me save me Lord I have never—*

She falls. Off the mule and out of herself. She is looking down, seeing what all around her see: the Holy Father writhing on the ground as though possessed, face whiter than his cassock, though that cassock not white at all from the waist down but blood and mud and how to know what is happening within, what without, what is real and what a vision from the devil.

In the midst of the blood and dirt and dust, the screaming and shouting and calls for exorcism, for recognition of a miracle, for stoning—a moment of perfect clarity. She hears the voice of Mary, which is not a voice at all, but a surge of strength in her loins and spine and heart that says, *Behold, I am the servant of the Lord; may it be done to me according to your word.* This great and holy force moving through her and of course of course of course God is here in the dirt, here with her opened body, its stench of shit and blood. He made it like this. Loves it like this. Lived for a time in one just like it. This breakable, tearable, messy, leaky, soft and hungry body.

Above her is held a tiny, glistening child. What a wonder, what a story, what a curious, miraculous, marvellous thing that here is a person where there was not.

The child is gone and faces contorted with rage and hatred loom but she is newborn herself, swaddled in peace.

This body was fated to end, as all bodies are. What a joy, what a marvel to know as she leaves it that she used it well. Let them have it, along with her titles and names, all useless things now.

Forgive them, Lord, they think they do this for You. They do not know—forgive them, forgive us all—that the only sacrament is Life and the sin is to waste it. Oh, Lord, what a final joy it is to know I did not. What a fine and curious and wondrous thing!

AUTHOR'S NOTE

ALTHOUGH SOME CHARACTERS in this novel share names and other qualities with historical figures and some events coincide with actual events, this is a work of fiction which draws on myths, legends, gossip, conjecture and the author's imagination at least as much as on historical sources and scholarship.

ACKNOWLEDGEMENTS

THE FIRST DRAFT of this project was written with the support of the Australia Council for the Arts. Three years later the novel was completed while I was the 2023 HC Coombs Creative Arts Fellow at the Australian National University. I am deeply grateful to Dr Lucy Neave and all at the ANU College of Arts and Social Sciences for the time, space and encouragement provided by this opportunity. Writing NSW provided a place to write (occasionally) and a sense of community (always).

Thank you Grace Heifetz for your integrity, kindness and courage-boosting; Jane Palfreyman for being the wise, staunch, giant-hearted publisher of my dreams; Federico Andornino for your enthusiasm and next-level brilliant editorial notes.

Thank you Ali Lavau for editing with such precision and curiosity, and Christa Munns for meticulous editing and organisational oversight. Thank you to everyone at Allen & Unwin and Sceptre for exemplary care at every stage.

Thank you Meredith Griffiths for long, wine-soaked conversations that helped me articulate vital elements of this novel and for helping me hold my nerve. Thank you Natasha Rai for being my first reader. I am so grateful for your perceptive, generous feedback and even more so for your friendship.

Thank you to my families (of birth, marriage and choice). Your unwavering love makes all things possible. Thank you Jeff for everything, always.